DEADMAN'S FLOAT

CRIME Á LA MODE, BOOK 1

CHRISTY BARRITT

To Buttons: the best thing we've ever found in a ditch. You keep us entertained and make us feel loved.

COMPLETE BOOK LIST

Squeaky Clean Mysteries:

#1 Hazardous Duty
#2 Suspicious Minds
#2.5 It Came Upon a Midnight Crime (novella)
#3 Organized Grime
#4 Dirty Deeds
#5 The Scum of All Fears
#6 To Love, Honor and Perish
#7 Mucky Streak
#8 Foul Play
#9 Broom & Gloom
#10 Dust and Obey
#11 Thrill Squeaker
#11.5 Swept Away (novella)
#12 Cunning Attractions
#13 Cold Case: Clean Getaway

#14 Cold Case: Clean Sweep

#15 Cold Case: Clean Break

#16 Cleans to an End (coming soon)

While You Were Sweeping, A Riley Thomas Spinoff

The Sierra Files:

#1 Pounced

#2 Hunted

#3 Pranced

#4 Rattled

The Gabby St. Claire Diaries (a Tween Mystery series):

The Curtain Call Caper

The Disappearing Dog Dilemma

The Bungled Bike Burglaries

The Worst Detective Ever

#1 Ready to Fumble

#2 Reign of Error

#3 Safety in Blunders

#4 Join the Flub

#5 Blooper Freak

#6 Flaw Abiding Citizen

#7 Gaffe Out Loud

#8 Joke and Dagger

#9 Wreck the Halls

#10 Glitch and Famous (coming soon)

Raven Remington

Relentless 1

Relentless 2 (coming soon)

Holly Anna Paladin Mysteries:

#1 Random Acts of Murder

#2 Random Acts of Deceit

#2.5 Random Acts of Scrooge

#3 Random Acts of Malice

#4 Random Acts of Greed

#5 Random Acts of Fraud

#6 Random Acts of Outrage

#7 Random Acts of Iniquity

Lantern Beach Mysteries

#1 Hidden Currents

#2 Flood Watch

#3 Storm Surge

#4 Dangerous Waters

#5 Perilous Riptide

#6 Deadly Undertow

Lantern Beach Romantic Suspense

Tides of Deception

Shadow of Intrigue
Storm of Doubt
Winds of Danger
Rains of Remorse

Lantern Beach P.D.
On the Lookout
Attempt to Locate
First Degree Murder
Dead on Arrival
Plan of Action

Lantern Beach Escape
Afterglow (a novelette)

Lantern Beach Blackout
Dark Water
Safe Harbor
Ripple Effect
Rising Tide

Crime á la Mode
Deadman's Float
Milkshake Up (coming soon)
Bomb Pop Threat (coming soon)
Banana Split Personalities (coming soon)

The Sidekick's Survival Guide

The Art of Eavesdropping

The Perks of Meddling

The Skill of Snooping (coming soon)

The Practice of Prying (coming soon)

Carolina Moon Series

Home Before Dark

Gone By Dark

Wait Until Dark

Light the Dark

Taken By Dark

Suburban Sleuth Mysteries:

Death of the Couch Potato's Wife

Fog Lake Suspense:

Edge of Peril

Margin of Error

Brink of Danger

Line of Duty

Cape Thomas Series:

Dubiosity

Disillusioned

Distorted

Standalone Romantic Mystery:

The Good Girl

Suspense:

Imperfect

The Wrecking

Sweet Christmas Novella:

Home to Chestnut Grove

Standalone Romantic-Suspense:

Keeping Guard

The Last Target

Race Against Time

Ricochet

Key Witness

Lifeline

High-Stakes Holiday Reunion

Desperate Measures

Hidden Agenda

Mountain Hideaway

Dark Harbor

Shadow of Suspicion

The Baby Assignment

The Cradle Conspiracy

Trained to Defend

Nonfiction:

Characters in the Kitchen

Changed: True Stories of Finding God through Christian Music (out of print)

The Novel in Me: The Beginner's Guide to Writing and Publishing a Novel (out of print)

CHAPTER ONE

Serena Lavinia stuck her head out the window as she drove down the weathered stretch of gravel beach road. It was summer, and tourists had flocked back to Lantern Beach like seagulls going after breadcrumbs.

And that was a good thing.

Because Serena had ice cream to sell. Lots and lots of ice cream.

"Get your ice cream sandwiches!" She leaned out and yelled the words over the sound of "Baa, Baa, Black Sheep" playing from her ice cream truck. "One for one dollar or five for five dollars!"

Serena had worked one summer in high school selling hot dogs for a minor league baseball team. Who knew that experience would come in handy now? There was definitely an art to live sales.

As Serena saw a family with three kids walking over, she pressed on the brakes and put her truck in Park. She plastered on her best smile, practicing being the aspiring businesswoman she knew she was, and greeted them.

"Good afternoon! Isn't it a lovely day here on Lantern Beach?"

The man looked uptight in his khaki shorts and polo shirt. It was obviously the family's first day here. Serena could spot the first-timers from a mile away.

Maybe by the end of his stay, the man would learn to untuck his shirt and live in a bathing suit, like most of the people on the island did.

He narrowed his eyes as he stared at the faded sign on the side of her ice cream truck, Elsa. Pictures of various treats covered it, along with the prices that, over the years, had been written with a marker, painted over, and then written again.

Improving the display was on Serena's list of things to do. She'd just installed a soft-serve ice cream dispenser so she could add floats and banana splits to her menu. Slowly but surely, she was making progress on her upgrades.

"What did you say the special is?" The man scratched his head as he stared at her.

"I've got a great deal for today only. Ice cream

sandwiches. One for one dollar or five for five dollars."

His eyes narrowed even more. "But . . ."

Before he could ask more questions, his three kids, which Serena guessed to all to be under the age of six, started jumping up and down and talking at the same time. "Ice cream, Daddy! Ice cream!"

He shook his head and pulled out his wallet. "Fine. We'll have five ice cream sandwiches."

"I knew you wouldn't be able to pass up that deal."

Serena winked before climbing into the back of her truck and sliding open the service window. She bent into the freezer below her and pulled out the frozen treats. With a big grin, she handed them to the children first, then to the mom and dad.

The dad paused after he paid. "I like the carhop outfit. It goes well with the whole ice cream truck thing."

Little did the man know that Serena dressed as a different character each day. It helped to keep people on their toes, among other things. Her revolving looks had become her signature in the area, and it gave locals something to talk about.

With one last smile and wave, Serena closed the window then continued on her route.

It was a Sunday afternoon near the end of June,

and the day promised to be a scorcher. Something about these sandy shores seemed to absorb the heat and make the air feel even hotter than the thermometer registered. But the breeze coming off the ocean worked hard to balance it all. Nature herself seemed to know the island needed some relief.

She turned at the end of the street and headed back, making a right onto the highway. This was her method. All right turns except at the very end where she had no choice but to make a left to continue the route down the opposite side of the street. Especially in the summer, the highway got busy and it was nearly impossible to make the turn across the road.

As she turned down another lane, marsh grass surrounded her on either side. Two houses were located at the end, but only one was occupied—as far as Serena knew, at least. No one ever bought anything from her on this street, but she hit it each day despite that.

At the end, as she turned around, a little dog scampered out from the marsh. It dropped something from its mouth and dashed toward the ice cream truck.

Serena threw on brakes before she collided with the canine.

The dog sat directly in front of Elsa, staring at Serena with his tongue out.

Out of curiosity, Serena climbed out of the truck and walked toward the animal. As she stooped down, the dog practically jumped into her arms, a ball of excitement and energy.

"My goodness," she murmured, rubbing the canine's head. "Aren't you a friendly boy?"

The dog continued to wiggle, acting as if Serena was his long-lost best friend.

She searched for a collar but found none. He must've gotten away from somebody. "Which one of these houses did you escape from?"

The dog stared back at her with big, brown eyes. If Serena had to guess—and she was no dog expert—this canine appeared to be some kind of terrier with coarse, brindle-colored hair and long, pointy ears. He looked to be around fifteen pounds.

She didn't normally consider herself a dog person, but this little guy was adorable.

"Do you want me to help you find your home?" Serena murmured.

The dog continued to wag his tail, a hyper mess in Serena's arms.

"I can help you do that." Serena let out a giggle as the dog licked her chin. "I can't have you out here wandering these roads. The highway is way too busy at this time of year."

She stood and glanced at the two houses in the

distance. It made sense to check them first and make sure the dog hadn't come from there. However, since the canine had walked through the marsh, there was a possibility he'd come from the next street over.

"Come on, boy. Let's go see if we can find your owner."

Serena left Elsa on the side of the lane, strands of "Boom, Boom, Ain't It Great to Be Crazy?" coming through the speakers. Elsa seemed to have a mind of her own and liked to choose her own songs. It sounded strange, and Serena didn't *really* believe the ice cream truck picked appropriate songs for the occasion. But that was how it seemed at times.

As she walked toward the end of the street, the dog trotted along beside her, almost as if they had been friends forever.

"It's a hot day for you to be out here." Talking to the dog came as naturally to her as talking to other people. Serena had never been shy and loved engaging with others. Hearing people's stories and opinions was part of what made life so interesting sometimes.

She reached the first house and climbed the steps to the front door. At the top, she didn't see a doorbell so she knocked. A moment later, a woman in her seventies answered and stared at Serena. Her gaze traveled up and down her outfit.

Serena knew what she was wearing was a little different. She had a poofy blue skirt that came to her knees, a black Polo trimmed in white that she'd tucked into it, and a ruffly white apron. She'd also found some Mary Janes to wear, as well as a circular blue hat that really pulled the whole look together.

She'd styled her dark hair in big curls that she'd pinned near her face, and her makeup looked classic, as if she'd stepped out of the fifties.

It was one of her better looks.

She didn't mind the stares. Besides, her Instagram followers loved seeing her revolving looks every day.

"Can I help you?" the woman asked, throwing a dishtowel over her shoulder.

Serena had seen her a couple of times on the island. The woman wasn't the type who went to many of the town's celebrations, but, if Serena remembered correctly, she did help with the annual crab fest every year.

"I found this dog wandering down the lane, and I was wondering if he was yours?" Serena asked.

The woman glanced down at the dog and shook her head, sneezing. "Not mine. I'm allergic. Even if I wasn't, I think terriers look like rats."

Serena glanced down at the puppy, who'd obediently sat by her feet.

"A rat? This cute little thing?" She shook off the

insult, trying to stay focused. "Do you happen to know if he might belong to your neighbor?"

"No one lives over there. It's owned by some guy up in New York, but he only comes down about once a year, if that. Haven't seen anyone over there in months."

Serena glanced down at the dog again and added, "Alrighty then, thanks for your help. I'll keep looking."

"I hope you're able to find the owner. I know they're probably upset to lose their pet. Then again, maybe that let that fleabag go." The woman leaned closer and scrunched her nose. "Rat dog."

Serena's mouth dropped open.

That was rude.

She shook her head at the woman before starting back toward her truck. What now?

Wait . . . she remembered seeing the dog drop something near the marsh before he'd trotted in front of her ice cream truck. Maybe it was a leash or a collar.

"Let's go see what you left over there, boy." Serena patted her leg to indicate the dog should follow.

She spotted the mystery object in the distance and walked toward it. As she got closer, she saw that it was a shoe. Some type of canvas loafer like the ones that were popular here on the beach.

"What is this?" Did it belong to the dog's owner? Perhaps the dog had been attempting to bring someone his shoes. Wouldn't that be cute?

Serena picked the loafer up, realizing that she probably wouldn't get much information from it. Still, if she found the dog's owner . . . maybe he'd want his shoe back as well.

She glanced at it again and sucked in a breath. Was that . . . blood?

She held the shoe closer and gasped. Yes. That was most definitely blood. It didn't appear to have come from the dog. There was too much of it. Large drips stained the top.

What exactly had happened to this dog's owner? And did Serena really want to find out?

Ten minutes later, Police Chief Cassidy Chambers showed up with two officers. As soon as Serena had seen the blood, she'd known she needed to call law enforcement and let them know what she'd found.

She and Cassidy were on a first-name basis. At least, Serena liked to think they were.

Cassidy put the shoe in a plastic evidence bag and

held it up. "The blood looks fresh. It's still red and not completely dry."

"I don't think this is from the dog," Serena said. "Do you?"

"Did you see any injuries on the animal?" Cassidy slid her sunglasses on as the bright sun bore down on them.

Serena looked at the puppy—she decided to call him Sprinkles for the time being—and shook her head. "No, I got the dog to roll over and to stand up on his back paws. He looks perfectly fine other than a few sand spurs in his hair."

"You did the right thing by calling us," Cassidy continued. "We're going to check this out. It could be as simple as someone who injured himself. Just because there's blood doesn't mean there was a crime."

Was it wrong that Serena almost hoped there was? It wasn't that she hoped someone had been malicious, causing pain to an innocent victim. But she loved the zing of excitement that coursed through her when it came to finding answers. That's why she also worked part-time for the island newspaper.

Between the ice cream truck and the newspaper she could pay her bills, though barely. She was finishing up her college degree online as well. She'd promised her mom that she would do so, and she hoped she would be able to one day use her business degree. But her mom was hoping she would use that education to do something a little more advantageous than selling ice cream here on this little island.

"What about the dog?" Serena asked, looking at Cassidy.

Cassidy knelt down and rubbed the dog on his head. "I can call animal control to hold him until we locate his owner."

Despair washed through Serena. This poor dog could *not* be put in the dog pound. It seemed like an atrocity to even think about it. Sprinkles was just too good for that.

"He can stay with me," Serena announced.

Cassidy raised an eyebrow. "Are you sure? Don't you have an ice cream route to do today?"

"Sprinkles is a great dog. I'm sure he'll stay in the ice cream truck without any problems."

"Sprinkles?"

Serena shrugged. "It just seemed like an appropriate name."

As if to agree, Sprinkles barked up at her and wagged his tail.

"I can see that. If you're sure you're okay with it, then you can keep the dog. If anybody calls about him, I'll let you know. Sound good?"

Serena smiled as she looked down at the dog. "Sounds great. Now, do you mind if I get back to my route?"

"Go right ahead. I'll call if we have any more questions."

Serena nodded and walked back to Elsa. She patted her leg again, and Sprinkles jumped into the truck beside her. She briefly wondered if this was against some kind of FDA standard, but she decided to ignore that question. All the ice cream in her freezers was prewrapped, so they should be fine.

Sprinkles sat in the passenger seat beside her, staring out the window with his tongue wagging.

"Are you thirsty, boy?"

The dog barked back at her.

Serena found a bowl left over from the time she'd done a special on banana splits. She took her bottle of water and poured some into the bowl. Sprinkles lapped at it until the container was dry.

"All right, let's get going," Serena announced.

She kind of liked having someone to talk to on her route. It beat talking to herself. She did that too, but people thought that was a little strange. Talking to Sprinkles was just another way of pretty much talking to herself but looking like she had more sanity intact.

"Maybe if we ride around, we'll find your owner." She put the truck in Drive.

Sprinkles barked, almost as if he understood what Serena had said.

As she pulled onto the next street, she kept her eyes open for any sign of someone searching for a dog. This was another one of those streets that usually didn't offer much business. But there were six houses down here, and a few of them were weekly vacation rentals, if Serena remembered correctly. Two of them were small cottages, two were midsize houses that were up on stilts, and two were newer builds, three stories high with swimming pools. It was an eclectic mix of everything here.

Her neighborhood in Michigan, where she had grown up, had a homeowner's association, and everything was always neat. All the houses had been uniform. Maybe some people liked how expected that was, but Serena much preferred the uniqueness of this area. There were so many personalities that fit together, even on the same street. She thought it was a good reflection of life.

Then again, she did dress as a different character every day, so maybe that was just unique to her.

Elsa seemed to be stuck on "Boom, Boom, Ain't It Great to Be Crazy?" and the song played in a loop. Even though Serena kept hitting fast forward, she knew it did no good. Elsa played what she wanted to play. It had always been that way.

Serena stuck her head out the window again and yelled her sales pitch to anybody who might be listening. "Ice cream sandwiches! One for one dollar or five for five dollars!"

As Serena pulled up to one of the midsize houses, a man stepped out and waved her down. He was probably in his thirties, with a prematurely fading hairline, a sun-kissed nose, and a lean build.

She stopped her truck and turned to him, putting on her sales lady smile. "Good day! Isn't it lovely here in Lantern Beach?"

She never got tired of saying that. Partly because the words were true. There was something about this island that she adored. She had to admit also that she'd practiced saying that line in the mirror over and over again, trying to perfect her sales pitch and smile.

"Look at that dog," he said. "He's a cutie."

Almost as if Sprinkles understood, he trotted across the seat to the window and happily accepted a head pat from the man.

"Do you, by any chance, recognize him?"

The man squinted. "No, I can't say I do. Is he lost?"

"I found him wandering around the next street over. I'm hoping I might find his owner."

He glanced up and down the lane. "I think all the houses here were full this past week. I know a couple of families were staying at that yellow house." He nodded to the big three-story residence across the street. "I'm trying to remember if I saw a dog with them."

"While I'm here, I guess it can't hurt to ask around, right?"

"No, I guess it can't."

"Before I do that, would you like something?"

"I'm not feeling like an ice cream sandwich, but I will have a Bomb Pop. Do you have any of those?"

"I sure do." Serena climbed into the back, handed him the popsicle, and he paid.

Then she put her truck in Drive again. But, instead of heading down the road, she pulled into the driveway across the street. This wasn't on her schedule. If she didn't bring in a certain amount of money per week, it was hard to pay her bills. The island had experienced a blackout a couple weeks ago, so she was still playing catchup.

Despite those hang-ups, she climbed out of the truck and approached the big, yellow house. Sprinkles followed on her heels. As they walked toward the stairs, the man who'd just bought the Bomb Pop jogged to catch up with her.

"Need some help?" he asked. "I'm assuming you're looking for the dog's owner."

She shrugged. She didn't really need help, but she supposed the man was just trying to be nice. "Sure."

"I have to admit, I'm kind of curious about what the inside of this house looks like. The people who were staying here last week had a tendency to stay up late blaring music and playing in the pool."

"The good news is you should have some new neighbors checking in later today, right?"

"That's right. I'm here for two weeks myself—just me and my surfboard. It's a beautiful place to find some Zen."

"It is," she said. "I'm Serena, by the way."

"Nice to meet you. I'm Lawrence Hollingshead. My friends call me Lawie."

They climbed the front steps to the place. Like many of the homes in the area, it was raised high on stilts to avoid damage from the floodwaters that were common to the area. Decks stretched around each story of the house, and Serena knew that the sunset views had to be astounding.

She rang the doorbell, but no one answered. There were no cars in the driveway either, so there was a good chance last week's renters had already gone. This place could very well be empty right now, waiting for the cleaning crew between visitors.

"Wouldn't it be horrible if someone left to go home and didn't realize they'd forgotten their dog?" Serena frowned at the thought of it. People's pets became like family to them.

"If that was the case, then they weren't very good dog owners." Lawrence shrugged. "But it still seems sad. Poor guy." He rubbed the dog's head as they lingered in front of the door.

"You didn't see the family leave?" Serena clarified.

"I didn't," he said, his voice having a touch of surfer twang. "But I've been at the beach for most of the morning."

"Let me make sure that nobody's in the back." Serena started around the deck, double-checking that this place was clear.

As she reached the back of the house, she glanced down at the swimming pool below.

She gasped.

A man was in the pool.

Floating facedown.

And looking very dead.

CHAPTER TWO

Serena saw the disbelief in Cassidy's gaze as the police chief stared at her as they stood on the deck where Serena had first spotted the dead body.

"So you just happened to wander up onto the deck of this house and just happened to see the dead body in the pool?" Cassidy asked.

"That's correct." Serena hugged Sprinkles closer. She'd never thought of herself as one to need a comfort blanket, but right now she could use all the puppy love she could get.

Still looking a touch perplexed, Cassidy looked back at Lawrence. "And who are you again?"

The man's face looked paler than it had earlier. "I'm Lawrence Hollingshead. I'm staying across the street. When Serena told me about the dog, I thought I would try to help her find the owner. Never expected this."

"Chief, look what I found," Officer Braden Dillinger called from the pool deck below.

Serena glanced down at what he held . . . a shoe.

A shoe that matched the one Sprinkles had been carrying earlier.

Serena held her dog even closer.

Part of her knew she should leave right now, that as soon as Cassidy cleared her to go, she should. But the other part of her needed answers. She needed to know what happened to the man. There had been blood on the shoe Sprinkles found. That seemed to indicate that there was more to this than an accident. In Serena's unstudied estimation, at least.

"Did you ever speak to your neighbors who were staying here?" Cassidy asked Lawrence.

"No, I didn't. We would nod and say hello to each other when we passed. Then again, I'm not even 100 percent sure that guy was one of the people renting this place. There were probably fifteen people in this house, so many that it was hard to tell one person from another. I'm guessing the rest of the crew left early this morning while I was at the beach."

"Today is checkout day so that is a possibility,"

Cassidy said. "Maybe we can ID him from his prints, or, if we're lucky, he'll have a driver's license on him. We'll call the management company also and find out the name and contact info of the person listed on the rental agreement."

Serena glanced down. Another officer pulled the dead body out of the water. As he did, a faint red line appeared in the water and then on the cement beside the pool.

A gunshot wound? Serena didn't think so. The rip in the man's shirt seemed to indicate a knife had sliced it. More blood seeped through the man's clothing, seeming to indicate the wound was deep.

"Maybe you shouldn't be seeing this." Cassidy moved in front of Serena to block her view.

The woman had always treated Serena like a younger sister. But, deep down inside, Serena knew the two of them had a connection. Cassidy had actually owned Elsa before she'd sold the ice cream truck to Serena.

"I'll be fine," Serena said.

"I don't think we need anything else from you. You can go, and we'll call you if any questions pop up." Cassidy turned her gaze to the man beside Serena. "Lawrence, I'm going to need some contact information from you as well."

Lawrence nodded, still looking pale, but he rattled off what she needed.

With one more glance at the scene, Serena stepped away. Maybe it was better if she didn't keep looking for Sprinkles' owner. Besides, his owner *could* be the dead guy.

And if he wasn't . . .?

Serena leaned down and rubbed the dog's head.

Right now, Sprinkles felt safer with Serena. And Serena felt safer with Sprinkles.

An hour later, Serena barged into the newspaper office, which also happened to be the home of Ernestine Sanders, the *Lantern Beach Outlook* editor. In small towns like this, real estate came at a premium, and it was more economical to run the online paper from her home.

"The story is mine," Serena announced.

"Story?" Ernestine looked up from the desk she'd set up in an old sunroom and stared at Serena, purple glasses perched on the end of her nose.

The woman was in her early sixties with salt-and-pepper hair that was cut in a neat bob. Her face was smooth and relatively wrinkle free, and she favored wearing linen pants with flowy shirts.

"There was a dead body found at one of the vacation rental houses here on the island. He was in the pool, and he had some kind of wound in his chest."

As if to affirm her story, Sprinkles barked beside her.

"A dog?" Ernestine's gaze went from Sprinkles back up to Serena, her eyes widening with confusion.

"It would take too long to explain right now. Can I please cover this investigation?" Sometimes Ernestine liked to keep the big stories for herself and made Serena simply do the footwork for her.

Ernestine frowned. "There's something I think you need to know."

"Okay. But first, can I? Please?" All she wanted was an answer.

"No, it's actually—"

"I can't tell you how much I want to do this. I was close to this crime scene, Ernestine. I can follow the story."

"Serena, I'm trying to tell you that—"

The next instant, Serena saw somebody walk toward them from the other room. Her entire body tensed. She had halfway expected it to be Clemson, Earnestine's "friend" and the town's doctor/medical examiner. Everybody knew there was more between the two than simple friendship.

But, instead, a strange man stood there. He was

on the shorter side, but fairly broad, with wire-frame glasses and short, light-brown hair. He had a bit of a nerd vibe, but not necessarily in a bad way. More like, in a smart way.

"Who are you?" Serena blurted, still eyeing him.

Part of her felt protective of Ernestine. The woman had agoraphobia and rarely left her house. That meant that Clemson and Serena were two of the few people she regularly interacted with. Strangely enough, Elsa's first owner—not Cassidy but the person before her—had actually been Ernestine's best friend.

"Serena, if you would let me talk . . ." Ernestine stared at her, obviously used to her antics.

Serena realized that she had been blathering and maybe even a touch rude. She started to defend herself but instead clamped her mouth shut. She should stop while she was ahead.

"Serena, this is my nephew, Webster Newsome."

Serena glanced at the man as he nodded at her, his hands stuffed into the pockets of his jeans. He was probably her age or a few years older. Twenty-six max.

"Nice to meet you, Webster," Serena said, getting the formalities out of the way.

"You too." His voice sounded deeper than Serena had expected.

"Webster is . . . the new newspaper editor."

Serena blanched, certain she hadn't heard correctly. "New editor? What do you mean? You're the editor."

"I think it's time for me to hang up my hat and retire," Ernestine said. "We need some new blood."

"So you hired this guy?" Serena blurted. "He doesn't know anything about the island."

"Serena—" Ernestine started, her eyelids drooping with possible exhaustion.

"I'm serious. How can someone be editor here if they're not even familiar with how this place operates?"

"Need I remind you that you were new here at one time too?" Ernestine's eyebrows shot up as she waited for Serena's response.

Serena crossed her arms, not ready to agree with Ernestine yet. Instead, she turned toward the newcomer. "What does he even know about the newspaper business?"

"I actually interned at *The New York Times,* and I worked full-time as a reporter for three years in DC. I later became an assistant editor in Richmond for two years, and then I decided I was ready for a change."

Serena tried to think of something snappy to say, but his résumé was impressive . . . unfortunately. "Well, I guess that's a good start. But that doesn't mean you know anything about managing the island newspaper. We have a delicate ecosystem here, and I'm not talking about our marshes or wetlands."

"Serena," Ernestine warned.

"What? I'm sorry. But I had no idea. I figured you were going to be the editor forever and you would eventually hand the reins over to—" Serena stopped herself, feeling her cheeks flush.

Had she been about to say herself? On a conscious level, she hadn't even realized that was a possibility. But, maybe, in the back of her mind, she'd assumed that one day Ernestine would let the newspaper's only reporter take over. It just made sense in the grand scheme of things.

Serena hadn't even had a clue that Ernestine had a nephew. The woman had never mentioned him.

"Look." Webster shifted, his expression full of what appeared to be well-practiced diplomacy. "I know this is coming as a surprise to you—"

Serena narrowed her eyes. "To say the least."

"But I promise you that I'm going to do my best to keep the torch going that my aunt has carried for so many years."

"And I'm going to be here to help him and to show him the ropes." Ernestine stood and put her arm around Webster. "I was hoping that you might be also."

Show him the ropes? That sounded awful. She could show him how to hang himself with a rope—professionally speaking, of course.

They waited for her response.

Serena shifted, feeling like she didn't have a choice. "I guess, but . . ."

Ernestine and Webster both stared at her, waiting for her to finish that thought.

Sprinkles barked up at her as if he understood.

Finally, Serena sighed. "It's not like I really have any say in this. But I really want to cover this murder. Can you give me that, at least?"

"I think this would be a great chance for you and Webster to get to know each other." Ernestine offered a satisfied nod. "So, yes, you can cover the murder. With Webster."

Serena narrowed her eyes and stared at the man. She didn't even know him, and yet he already felt like an enemy. He was in her territory, intruding on a space she'd earned the right to.

She leaned down and rubbed Sprinkles' head. She herself felt a bit like a dog letting out a soft, warning growl to let someone know this turf had been claimed.

Webster didn't seem to notice.

"Why don't we start now?" Webster asked. "There's no time like the present, right?"

Serena forced a smile. She wasn't going to enjoy this. Not one bit.

CHAPTER THREE

"I can drive," Webster said as he and Serena stepped outside into the bright sunshine.

Serena still felt trapped, as if she'd had no say in any of this—because she hadn't. And she resented the man for that fact. Plus, she'd still need to finish her route later.

"The dog goes with us," she announced.

She wasn't going to make this easier than necessary for him. She'd had to claw her way to the top—and by the "clawing her way" she meant that she'd stumbled into the job and not let go. And by "the top" she meant as the online newspaper's only reporter—because no one else had wanted the job.

But still.

Webster glanced down at the dog. "What's his name?"

"Sprinkles."

"Sprinkles? I like that. He's more than welcome to ride in the car with us."

Well, that tactic hadn't worked. Serena had pictured him as the type who'd want to keep the canine out of his space, as the kind who liked things to be overly neat and tidy.

Serena would have to keep thinking of ways to scare him off before he ever really started.

She climbed into the passenger side of a midsize sedan with shiny rims and dark-blue paint untouched by the sand and saltwater—for now. The elements were hard on vehicles around here. Serena pictured Webster as the type who would be outside every day washing his car and trying to keep it looking clean.

She picked up Sprinkles and held the dog in her lap as she closed the door. The windows were down, and the dog's head went outside again, like it was his most favorite thing in the whole wide world to do.

Serena had tried it once. It was pretty fun.

"So, my aunt tells me you also drive the ice cream truck." Webster started the car but made no move to leave yet. Instead, he nodded to Elsa, which Serena had haphazardly parked in the shade across the lawn.

"That's right. A lot of people around here have to

have more than one job in order to make ends meet." Although, if Serena had gotten a job as newspaper editor, that might not be a problem anymore. It was just as well. At least, when she drove the ice cream truck, it let her get some of her people fix out of the way. Talking was her love language.

"I'm guessing you dress like a carhop because you sell ice cream?" Webster continued, glancing at her outfit.

Oh, he was in for a surprise. But maybe Serena would let him figure that out the hard way. She liked to keep people guessing.

"That's right," Serena said.

"Okay then." His hand went to the gearshift, as if ready to put the vehicle into Drive. "Where should we start? Should we go back to the scene of the crime?"

"We can, but Cassidy won't be happy to see me if we do."

"Who is Cassidy?" A knot formed on his brow.

"I figured you'd done your research by now," Serena said, feeling slightly satisfied with herself. "Cassidy Chambers is our police chief here in town."

"And the two of you are on a first-name basis?"

Serena shrugged. "As far as I'm concerned, we are."

He stared at Serena for a moment before letting

out a little chuckle. He had no idea what to do with her, did he? "Okay. I see. Well, I was actually hoping I could get a good feel for the island. Maybe we should do that now until the crime scene is cleared and the police chief will talk to us. I can make sure that my aunt pays you for your time."

Getting paid for her time was a benefit. Serena nodded. "Fine. I can show you around town."

Certainly Webster realized that his aunt couldn't show him around town. Ernestine had only left her home a total of five times since Serena had known her.

"How long have you lived here?" Webster asked, making no effort to pull away. Thankfully, the live oak trees that graced the area provided some shade until the car cooled off.

"About two years now. I've gone back to Michigan a couple times, but I finally decided on staying in Lantern Beach for good. There's something about this island that I connect with, that's become part of me."

"It's nice to feel like you're a part of something." A certain wistfulness feathered his voice.

"And why in the world would you give up your job in Richmond to come here?" It made sense for someone like Serena to do it. A free-spirited wanderer was buried down deep inside her. But someone like Webster . . . he seemed like the type who wanted a stable job, a steady paycheck, and the perfect little American life, complete with a white picket fence.

"It's a long story," he said quickly, suddenly not seeming as chatty.

Serena knew there had to be more to his story, but she didn't press. Not right now, at least. Instead, she asked, "When did you get here?"

"Last night. It was a long drive so I slept in this morning. It's not something I do very often, and my aunt is an early riser, so I didn't sleep as well as I'd hoped." He pushed his glasses up higher on his nose and put his car into Drive, as if talking about himself made him uncomfortable. "So where should we start?"

He'd changed the subject. He probably thought Serena hadn't noticed, but she had. She would let it slide for now, though.

Instead, she let out a sigh before pointing at the road in the distance. "Well, let's start with a right-hand turn . . ."

An hour later, Serena had shown Webster everything on the island, from the lighthouse at the southern tip up through the fishing pier, then the boardwalk and retail area. They'd continued north all the way up to where the church was located. It had been a quick tour of the island, but she'd tried to hit all the major hotspots.

Just like any good reporter, Webster had asked a lot of questions and seemed interested in most things.

When she was done, Serena realized that she really needed to walk Sprinkles so he could use the bathroom. She pointed to a public beach access point. "Do you mind pulling off over here?"

"Sure. Maybe by the time we take a little walk with Sprinkles, the crime scene will be clear and we can talk to the police chief."

The man seemed so happy and optimistic. Serena usually liked happy and optimistic. Except that Webster's optimism seemed to contradict her grumpiness right now. She didn't quite know what to do about that.

Webster found a spare bag in his glove compartment and put it in his pocket. "Just in case Sprinkles leaves a little present."

Serena barely knew the man, but he already seemed to think of everything. More resentment grew in her. Serena knew it was ridiculous, but that didn't stop the emotion from rearing its ugly head.

This man was intruding on her life, and she didn't like it.

Despite that, she climbed out with her dog.

Even though canines were supposed to be on a leash on the beach, Serena didn't have a leash yet for Sprinkles. The dog seemed like he was going to follow her everywhere, so hopefully it wouldn't be a problem.

As soon as Serena crossed over the sand dune, an immediate peace filled her. There was something about being here on the ocean that soothed her soul. The reaction wasn't unique to her. People came from all over the country to experience some of this serenity.

Thankfully, some of the crowds on this stretch of beach had thinned out. No doubt people were heading back to their rentals in time for a late dinner or other evening activities they'd planned.

With Sprinkles by her side, she started walking down the shore toward a pier in the distance.

"On Tuesdays the community likes to gather here at the pier," she explained, trying some small talk. "People bring their hammocks and string them up between the posts. There's usually live music and some food trucks and even a few bonfires. It's really nice."

"I will have to check it out sometime while I'm

here, then." Webster walked beside her, his hands stuffed into the pockets of his jeans.

"While you're here?" She caught onto the meaning of his words, and hope surged in her. "That makes it sound like you're not going to stay for an extended period."

A slight red tinged his cheeks. "I didn't say that."

"But your words implied it."

He shrugged. "I plan on staying in town for a while. A good while."

Serena fought disappointment. She'd be lying if she said his words hadn't felt like a dagger bursting her hope-filled balloon.

As Sprinkles hurried ahead, sniffing dune grass and following some kind of scent, Serena and Webster continued to stroll behind him. The sand was soft at their feet, and the sound of the waves seemed to wash away any problems.

Except the fact that Webster was here. But there was nothing Serena could do about that now. Eventually, he'd probably realize this wasn't the place for him. She just needed to give it some time.

"So a murder here on Lantern Beach?" Webster said. "I figured when I took this job that it was going to be pretty boring."

"You might be surprised just how many things happen here in Lantern Beach," Serena said. "I'm not easily surprised, yet this place has thrown me for a loop more than once."

"I think I'm going to like it here."

Sprinkles stopped by something on the sand. When Serena saw him sniffing, she instantly tensed, remembering seeing that dog with a bloody shoe. Had he found something else?

But as Serena reached him, she saw that somebody had made a lovely heart out of broken seashells. The display was probably four feet by four feet, and it was surprisingly untouched by any tourists who'd been out here today. Maybe that was because it was close enough to the sand dune that nobody had disturbed it.

"Wow." Serena paused beside it. "This is really beautiful. Someone obviously put a lot of time and energy into it."

Her words were true. These shells hadn't haphazardly been placed in a heart shape. All of the lines were perfectly even and neatly layered. The colors of the shells somehow made it look like the heart had a shadow behind it. She pulled out her phone and snapped a picture.

"I agree," Webster said. "It's very nice."

"A lot of people come to the beach to heal," Serena said. "When I see this, that's what it makes me think of. Healing and peace."

"Did you come here to heal?"

Serena turned her head toward Webster. Did he really ask that question? It seemed so personal. She wanted to brush the inquiry off, to pretend like he was totally out of line. There were some things she just didn't want to talk about. "I guess we all leave things behind," she finally said. "Oh look, Sprinkles seems to have done his business. I think it's time that we go talk to Cassidy now."

Subject changed.

Because even though Serena thought of herself as an open book, there were some chapters she'd prefer to skip.

CHAPTER FOUR

"So, Cassidy Chambers, our police chief, looks like she could be a lifeguard instead of head of law enforcement," Serena said as they parked in front of the police station and then walked toward the door. "But she's actually pretty tough. I just thought I'd give you that warning. If you make any *Baywatch* references, Cassidy very well could kick you in the shin and make it look like an accident."

Webster nodded, looking unruffled. "I think I can handle her."

Serena shrugged. She'd let him find out for himself. Cassidy could be the nicest person in the world, but you didn't want to get on her bad side. She was relentless when it came to tracking down criminals on the island.

Before Serena could say anything else, Webster pulled open the door to the police station and charged inside like he owned the place. Serena scrambled behind him, Sprinkles in her arms.

Serena couldn't wait to see this. She loved it when Cassidy put people in their place. Well, she didn't love it when Cassidy put *her* in place. But anybody else, she did—especially someone like Webster, who didn't belong here on the island.

Serena really shouldn't think like that, yet she couldn't shake the urge for this man to leave. Not yet, at least.

The editor job should've been hers. She had a feeling Webster wouldn't last long here on this island. Then she could take the job that was rightfully hers.

Webster charged up to reception desk. "Hi, my name is Webster, and I'm the new editor of the *Lantern Beach Outlook*. I'd like a word with the police chief, please."

Serena raised her eyebrows. He sounded tough. Surprising.

A moment later, Cassidy stepped out. Her gaze went from Webster to Serena and back to Webster. "I'm Police Chief Chambers. What can I do to help you?"

"I was hoping to have a word with you."

"Come this way." Cassidy led them the short distance back to her office, and they each took a seat across from her at her desk.

Serena sat with Sprinkles in her lap, waiting for Cassidy to say something about having a dog in the building.

She didn't.

"I'd really like to get a statement from you about what happened at the rental house today," Webster started, diving right in.

"We're trying to put together a press release right now."

"I'm not really interested in a press release. Like I said, as the editor of the local newspaper, I'd like to get an interview with you about today's events."

Serena's eyebrows shot up. This man had transformed from mild and meek Clark Kent to Superman. She hated to admit it, but she was kind of impressed at how hardnosed he sounded.

"Well, Mr. Webster." Cassidy laced her fingers together in front of her as she sat at the desk. "That's not really the way things work around here."

"I am a reporter, and you can't deny me my first amendment right."

She leveled her gaze with him. "I'm certain that I can keep information from you until we learn the identity of this man and notify his family."

Webster leaned back. "Then you can tell us other details about the crime. Maybe we can work together. You give me information, I run the article, and someone might come forward with more information."

"Look," Cassidy started, some of the friendliness leaving her voice. "I know you're new here and still trying to learn the ropes. I can appreciate that. But a newspaper editor is not going to tell me how to do my job. Do you understand that?"

Serena held her breath, waiting to see how Webster would react. This was better than she'd ever thought. Cassidy was going to run this guy off before Serena could.

"I understand and respect your position." Webster appeared totally unflustered. "But you need to respect my position too. If there's a killer here on this island, the community needs to know. I have other ways I can find out."

Cassidy raised her chin. "I wouldn't suggest you sticking your nose where it doesn't belong. If you interfere with my investigation, there will be consequences."

As if agreeing, Sprinkles let out a little bark.

Neither Webster or Cassidy seemed to notice.

"I don't intend on messing up your investigation," Webster said. "But I'm not afraid to do my own either. When you're ready to give your statement, I would appreciate a call." Webster reached into his pocket and pulled out a card. Then he stood and left it on her desk. "Come on, Serena. Let's go."

Serena glanced over her shoulder at Cassidy before leaving the office. She shrugged, letting Cassidy know that she had nothing to do with how Webster had acted.

Serena still wasn't sure if she was impressed or put off. But right now, she had to admit she was feeling pretty fascinated.

Serena braced herself for whichever side of Webster she was about to experience as they climbed back into the car.

But it quickly became clear that he was still in Superman mode.

"Tell me what you know about this guy," he said as he cranked the engine. The laid-back tourist was long gone, and a big city reporter had taken his place.

"I don't know what to say." Serena's mind raced to come up with something reasonable.

"How old do you think this man was?"

"If I had to guess, I'd say mid-thirties."

"What did he look like?"

"Caucasian. Dark hair. Thin."

"What did you hear the police chief say when she came to the crime scene?"

"Well . . . this man had some kind of wound on his abdomen. I think he was stabbed."

"Keep going. Tell me everything. No detail is too small."

Man, this guy could really be intense when he wanted to. Serena felt like she was being interrogated. "The neighbor told me there were probably fifteen people staying at the house where the victim was found, but those renters must've left this morning. I'm trying to think of what else . . . Oh, one of his shoes was found by the pool deck."

"And the other one?"

She rubbed Sprinkles' head. "The dog had it when I first saw him."

He jerked his head toward her. "What?"

"Sprinkles had it in his mouth. And there was blood on it. Fresh blood. Based on that, I guess we can assume this man died this morning. He must have been stabbed and pushed into the pool."

"You're really confusing sometimes, you know that? I can't figure you out. Are you a caricature or an all-star investigator? I'm still not sure."

"I have been told before that I'm confusing." So many times, for that matter.

Webster cleared his throat and turned back to the road ahead, almost as if he hadn't intended on getting personal. "We need to find out everything we can about this guy. Who told you that there were fifteen people staying at the house?"

"The neighbor. His name was Lawrence, I believe."

"Let's go pay Lawrence a visit."

Serena thought she was aggressive when it came to these things. But, apparently, she wasn't. Not when compared to Webster.

But she couldn't ignore the zing of excitement that rushed through her blood either. She was investigating a murder.

This was going to be interesting.

CHAPTER FIVE

Lawrence Hollingshead was just walking in from the beach when Webster and Serena arrived. His nose was sunburned, and his skin had sand stuck to it, but he looked just as friendly as he had earlier.

Webster parked in front of his house, and they climbed out to approach him.

Serena cleared her throat as they paused near his house, stopping him before he could reach his outdoor shower. "I don't know if you remember me from earlier . . ."

"How can I forget?" Lawrence looked at Serena's outfit before giving her a knowing look.

She shrugged. She supposed it was pretty unforgettable.

"I want to introduce you to my . . . friend Webster.

He is the editor of the *Lantern Beach Outlook,* and he's here investigating what happened earlier."

Lawrence extended his hand. "Nice to meet you. Lawrence Hollingshead. Down here from Pennsylvania for two weeks. Never expected this kind of excitement, though."

"No one ever does." Webster's gaze remained focused and professional. "I was wondering if you'd seen anything strange up and down the street since you've been in town."

Lawrence rubbed his chin and stared off into the distance. "Strange? I don't think so. Like I was telling the ice cream lady here, there were a lot of people at that house across the street, and they liked to stay up late blaring their music. But there wasn't much else going on here."

"Was there anybody out of the ordinary that you noticed around here?" Webster continued.

"There's the ice cream lady." Lawrence nodded at Serena and let out a throaty, teasing chuckle. "And, of course, the cops came earlier today. The dogcatcher did come up and down the street a few times recently also."

Serena glanced down at Sprinkles and rubbed the dog's head. There would be no dogcatcher for this dog. Had he been out here looking for her little stray?

She caught herself mid-thought. Sprinkles was

not *her* dog. Somebody else was probably looking for this precious little canine, and Serena would be smart not to get too attached. She was solo on this cold journey of selling frosty treats to overheated beachgoers.

"That's good to know. If you think of anything else, please call me." Webster pulled one of his handy-dandy business cards from his pocket and handed it to Lawrence.

Serena made a mental note that she needed to get herself some of those.

"Of course." Lawrence held up the card between two fingers. "No problem."

As they walked away from the man, Serena turned to Webster. "What are you thinking now?"

Webster pushed up his glasses. "Now I want to see the crime scene."

Serena remembered being on that deck, looking down at the pool. She shuddered when she remembered the dead body. It wasn't every day she saw one of those. But she didn't argue with him.

There were no police there to stop them from climbing the steps up to the deck to peer at the pool area.

"Going into the pool area might be crossing some boundaries," Webster explained. "There is police tape there, after all. But there's no police tape up here on the deck. Let's see if we can find anything."

Serena stared down at the pool as they climbed the wooden steps. This time, she was thinking a little more clearly than earlier. She pictured the police officer pulling that body from the water and placing the John Doe on the side of the pool. Pictured the water and blood that had spread on the concrete around him.

She squinted. On the other side of the pool, she spotted a dark spot on the cement.

Water would have dried by now. Was that . . . ?

"Blood?" she blurted.

Webster glanced at her. "What?"

She pointed to the area she was talking about and tried to articulate more clearly. "Is that blood?"

At once, she pictured what happened here. That man must have gotten into an argument with somebody. As a result, he'd probably been stabbed. His body had been pushed into the pool, where he'd later been found.

Had one of his shoes fallen off in the process? And, if so, how had Sprinkles ended up getting it?

There were a lot of questions they didn't have answers to.

Webster pointed at the sign for Seaside Vacations,

the realty company that managed the property. "Do you know anybody who works there?"

"Actually, one of my neighbors is a housecleaner for them."

His eyes lit. "Great. This is your assignment for tonight. I need to see if you can find out the name of the family that was staying here. Can you do that for me?"

"I can try—"

"I didn't say try." Webster leveled his Superman-like gaze. If she wasn't careful, he would start shooting his laser-beam eyes at her in a moment. "I need you to do it. Understand?"

Serena opened her mouth before shutting it again. Had he really just tried to act like the boss of her?

Ernestine never talked to her like that. Serena's old editor had let Serena take her own pace when it came to writing these articles.

But Webster's stare made it clear that he was serious.

Was he the type who wanted a clean slate when he started a new job? She'd heard stories of people like that, people who fired the whole workforce when they took over in order to hire their own people.

"I'll do my best," she finally said.

Webster nodded, as if satisfied with her answer.

"Great. Let's check in with each other in the morning. There's a restaurant I've heard about here called The Crazy Chefette. My aunt's friend Clemson was talking about it. Can you meet there at eight?"

"I can, but I usually do my ice cream route around lunchtime and—"

"That will be perfect then. I'll see you at eight at The Crazy Chefette. Now, let me get you back to your truck, and I'm going to get back to work. We've got to get a jumpstart on this. It's our civic duty."

Serena parked her ice cream truck in front of the little camper she called home. Her aunt Skye had lived here before, but Skye had recently gotten married and, of course, moved in with her husband, Austin. When that happened, Serena had begun renting the space from them.

The living quarters was actually perfect for her. It was retro and mostly white with a teal stripe running down the side. A deck ran the length of it, complete with a hammock strung in the corner. Inside, there was enough space for a bed, mini-kitchen, and dining room table that converted into a couch. Serena's aunt had used stencils to create a black-and-white design on the old vinyl floor, and the kitchen cabinets had been painted sea-glass blue.

It might seem strange to some people that Serena lived in a campground, but it wasn't entirely unusual for this area. The cost of housing could be astronomical in the vacation community.

Besides, Serena kind of liked it here with the quirky mishmash of residents. It was simple and she had everything she needed. Plus, the Pamlico Sound was just a short walk away, and the sunsets there were nothing short of amazing.

After going inside to get a bowl of water for Sprinkles, Serena lay in the hammock. Sprinkles sprang up beside her and turned over on his back, almost like a baby might. She rubbed the dog's head, feeling like the two of them had been buddies for much longer than they really had.

How had Sprinkles gotten that bloody shoe? And who did Sprinkles belong to? Why isn't anybody out looking for their family pet?

Serena had fully been expecting to get a call from Cassidy saying that Serena needed to bring the dog by for the owners to pick up. But no one had called. If Serena had lost a dog like Sprinkles, she'd search night and day until she found him.

As her hammock swung back and forth with the breeze, Serena's thoughts went to Webster.

As soon as the man's image crossed her mind, her muscles tensed. He'd waltzed into town taking her job, and now he was like a tornado as he tried to find answers.

Serena wasn't sure which side of him she was more fascinated with. The humble and meek side? Or the superhero side?

Of course, she didn't have much room to complain about people having different sides. She was as complex as a twenty-layer cake like her mom used to make.

And she liked it that way.

It kept people guessing.

She rubbed Sprinkles' head for a few more minutes. Night had fallen, and the stars that stretched above were glorious. There was hardly any light out here to obstruct the view. She could even see the Milky Way dancing across the sky in all its glory.

Coming to Lantern Beach was one of the best things Serena could have done. She was the kind of girl who took life day by day. Could she stay here forever? She didn't know. But for right now, this worked for her.

Her mind wandered back to Webster again. Not that she wanted it to. Her mind just seemed to have a mind of its own. Her mind had a mind of its own? What kind of thought was that?

Regardless of her illogical logic, Serena remembered his assignment. She hadn't appreciated Webster's approach, but she understood where he was coming from. They needed to find out who was staying in that house if they wanted to learn the identity of their John Doe.

She stretched quickly before standing from the hammock. Sprinkles jumped down beside her and stared up at her, waiting.

"Come on boy," she said. "Let's go find Kai."

She walked two rows over and spotted Kai Wilson sitting outside on her porch deck husking some corn, the only light that of the strung-up bulbs crisscrossing on ropes above. The woman had long blonde hair with dreadlocks. She had a Rastafarian vibe, with tanned skin that was prematurely wrinkled. She wore colorful headbands and sleeveless shirts that showed her muscular arms.

Kai's eyes lit up when she spotted Serena.

"Serena girl. What brings you this way? And who is this that you have with you?" Kai eyed the dog and clicked her tongue to call him over.

"This is my temporary dog, Sprinkles."

"Sprinkles is a very cute boy." She bent down and patted the dog's head. Sprinkles ate up the attention and leaned into Kai's touch before coming back to Serena's side.

"What brings you by?" Kai asked, continuing to work on her corn. She had three bushels on the ground, and another basket full of shucked corn.

"I have a few quick questions for you," Serena started, leaning against an old barrel that served as a stool. "Do you know that big three-story yellow house on Seashell Lane at the north end of the island?"

"Yes, yes. Of course. That one's a real bugger to clean. It's so big that it takes three of us to get it turned over in time for the new guests to come."

That didn't surprise Serena. "Did you hear what happened there today?"

Kai looked up, her motions slowing. "About the body in the pool? Yes, yes. I heard about that too. Nobody can believe it."

Serena shifted, unsure how to ask her next question. So she just dove in. "Were you supposed to clean up there today, by chance?"

"I was. My manager called at the last minute and told me to leave it alone. Why are you asking?"

"I was wondering when you were given your assignments to clean, if you're given the names of the families who were staying there?"

She tossed another cob of corn into the basket. "I am. Every once in a while, someone tries to sneak in and pretend like they're a guest when they're not.

Now, we have the names of the guests who are leaving and the names of the guests who are coming. But I still don't understand why you're asking."

"I was hoping you might be able to tell me the name of the family that just left."

Kai's eyes narrowed, and she paused, taking a sip of iced tea from a mason jar. "Why do I have a feeling that there's more to this story?"

"I was the one who found the body," Serena said. "I guess I'm just kind of curious about what's going on."

"Oh, yes, yes. That makes sense. I'll tell you what. I'll see what I can find out. That information isn't on me right now, but I did leave it in my locker at the management company. I'll call you tomorrow when I see it."

Serena nodded. That had been easier than she thought. "Thank you so much, Kai."

"No problem, Serena. But I will take a Bomb Pop for my efforts."

"One Bomb Pop coming up." Serena grinned. It is amazing what a little ice cream could buy.

CHAPTER SIX

Serena woke up bright and early the next morning and got dressed in her outfit of the day.

Every Friday evening, she planned her entire wardrobe for the upcoming week. That was why on Sunday she'd worn her carhop outfit. Today, her outfit of choice just happened to be a . . . dogcatcher.

She couldn't help but think about how appropriate that was.

She donned the all-white coveralls and matching white cap. To top it off, she'd found a long metal pole at a local thrift store that looked like an animal catching device, especially after she'd glued a loop of rope at the end.

After taking one last look in the mirror, she glanced at the dog faithfully sitting at her feet.

"Hey, Mocha." Serena decided this morning that the moniker was a better name for the dog than Sprinkles. "Don't worry. I would never use this pole thing on you."

Mocha looked at her and wagged his tail.

The dog had slept at the foot of her bed all night, as if he had done it a million times before. He was pretty much the perfect dog with his pointy ears and intelligent eyes. If the owner didn't step forward, Serena would have the dog at least two more days. The island vet was only here once a week, on Thursdays.

When Dr. Varsha arrived, Serena could check to see if the dog had been microchipped.

Part of Serena hoped he hadn't. She kind of liked having Mocha around.

After getting ready, she pulled out her phone and did a quick video for her Instagram and YouTube accounts. Not many people knew it, but online she went by the name of "I Am Quick Change," and she had fifty thousand followers now. She had enough influence that a few companies had even started sending her products for endorsement.

It was kind of fun. Serena capitalized on her ability to change her looks by utilizing different clothing, various makeup techniques, and self-taught hairstyles. Every day she tried to do something different to keep her fans entertained. She'd had no idea it would be so popular.

"How about if you and I go on a quick walk before we meet bossy Webster."

Mocha barked in agreement.

Instead of taking the ice cream truck, Serena decided to walk across the street to the beach. She could follow the shore, and eventually she would arrive at The Crazy Chefette.

She preferred walking or riding her bike over taking the ice cream truck all over town in her off hours. Mocha seemed game for a walk as he trotted along beside her.

She did, however, decide to leave her dog catcher props at home for now.

As she stepped onto the sandy shore, just as always, she felt right at home. This area just gave her so much peace. She wouldn't trade that peace for anything—certainly not for the stress of living in her upper middle-class neighborhood back in Michigan.

Serena had tried so hard to fit in. Now she was just happy to be herself—whatever form that might take.

Just up ahead, she saw some more shells that had been artistically arranged.

Her heartrate quickened.

This wasn't the same heart image she had seen

yesterday. Whoever had designed that must have created something new last night.

Serena couldn't wait to see what it was.

With Mocha trotting beside her, she reached the informal exhibit and glanced down. Her heart caught at what she saw. Someone had arranged seashells in the shape of a huge sunshine with a gigantic smile.

Seeing that made a grin spread across her face.

She pulled out her camera and took a picture. These were too pretty not to document.

Somebody less skilled might have made the circle uneven or not paid attention to the hue of the shells. But whoever had designed this had. The arrangement was going to bring everyone who saw it a lot of happiness. It was a reminder of hope.

Even carefree Serena could use a dose of hope at times.

Serena glanced at her watch. She had only ten minutes until she was supposed to meet Webster. She better get a move on if she was going to make it on time.

As she walked, she waved to a few early morning people who had come out. A couple people did yoga. A few people jogged. Still others just sat on the shore and watched waves and the sun rising higher in the sky. Although the sun had come up almost two hours ago, the sky was still tinged with pink and light yellow.

She clicked her tongue, and Mocha began following her. As they reached the boardwalk area, they cut across the dunes, through a parking lot, and then crossed the street. She walked a couple blocks and finally arrived at The Crazy Chefette.

Her friend Lisa Dillinger owned this place, and it was a favorite among locals and foodies alike. Lisa enjoyed putting together clever, creative recipes that kept the taste buds guessing. The pink and white building looked cheerful and inviting.

Right before she walked inside, Kai called her with an update. When Serena ended the call, satisfaction rang through her.

She had something to share with Webster.

If she decided to share it.

Serena walked into the restaurant, right on time.

Stepping inside, she spotted Webster sitting at a corner booth with some coffee in front of him. He looked as prim and proper as ever. Even though they were in a beach town, he was wearing some dark-wash jeans with a solid gray T-shirt.

She was going to have to teach him a thing or two

about island living—starting with the fact he needed to loosen up.

She slid into the booth across from him and instructed Mocha to sit at her feet. She wasn't sure if dogs were allowed inside or not, but it was better to be ignorant than ask for permission. In her estimation, at least.

"Serena." Webster glanced up and down, soaking in her outfit. "You look . . . different today."

"Do I?" She decided to mess with his head just a little bit more. It was so much fun.

"And you brought Sprinkles with you. Inside the restaurant."

"It's Mocha," she corrected.

"But I thought you said yesterday—"

"It's Mocha," she repeated.

Webster stared at her for another moment before offering a brief nod and clearing his throat. "So, what's good here?" He lifted up a laminated menu.

"Everything. Lisa Dillinger—she's the owner—is a great chef. She always puts her own unique twist on all the food. I think you'll like whatever you get."

"Great. Because I was thinking about trying the shrimp and grits with . . . mango?"

"That's always a favorite. I, for one, am going to get the avocado toast topped with strawberries and balsamic vinegar, bacon on the side."

He lowered his menu. "That sounds . . . interesting. And like something you've gotten before, if I had to guess."

"I suppose it is." Sometimes that fact even surprised Serena. She liked to keep things mixed up in so many areas of her life. But when it came to what she ate? She pretty much stuck to what she knew she liked.

"So, what did you find out?" Webster asked after they ordered their food.

"You do like to get right to the point, don't you?" He didn't waste any time transforming into his alter ego, Serena noted.

"Well, time is money, right?"

Serena pulled in a deep breath. "I was able to talk to my friend Kai who works for the vacation management company. She told me Richard and Junita Jones, the family who was staying at that house, were from New Jersey. Approximately fifteen people were supposed to be there. No pets."

"Good work."

Before they could continue, a couple people came over to chat and meet Webster. By the time Serena finished introducing him to some locals, their food had come. The spicy scent of Webster's meal mixed with the fresh scent of orange juice and the savory smell of bacon.

Serena muttered a quick prayer before digging in. "What about you? Did you learn anything new?"

"As a matter fact, I did learn a few things." Webster held up his phone. "The police department put out a press release."

Her pulse spiked. "And?"

"It turns out the man who died is named Paul Witherspoon, from upstate New York. He was thirty-six years old, and he died from a stab wound to the chest, just like you suspected." Webster showed her a picture of the man on his phone. "The man's wallet was still on him, but I suspect that only his driver's license and some cash was inside. In other words, no clues to his murder, at least from what I can surmise."

Surmise? Serena wasn't sure she'd ever heard anyone use that word. She kind of liked it.

Serena's pulse spiked. "Was this Paul guy staying with the Jones family?"

"From what I can tell, no, he wasn't. But I haven't been able to ascertain where he was staying here on the island." He lifted his fork and tried the first bite of his breakfast. "This *is* good."

"Told you. Lisa never lets me down." Serena smiled before turning the conversation back to the case. "Nobody has come forward as a friend or relative, I take it?"

"My understanding is no, no one has come forward. The information on the man is vague. But now that you have a name and number of the family who are staying there, I plan on giving them a call to see if they recognize him."

"I'm sure that Cassidy's already done that."

Webster shrugged. "She may have, but that doesn't mean she'll share the information with me."

"Smart thinking, because she probably won't." Serena took another bite of her toast.

"Okay, so we have the guy's name, age, and hometown. We know how and where he died. It still seems like there are a lot of missing pieces, though."

"So how are we going to find those missing pieces? I mean, I have to do my ice cream route, of course. But I'm assuming we're going to keep investigating."

"You assumed correctly. I'd like for you to talk to Cassidy and see if she'll share anything with you."

Serena raised her brow and sneaked a piece of her toast crust to Mocha beneath the table. "After the way you talked to her yesterday, I doubt that she will."

"I was just being direct and professional." He pushed his glasses up.

"You can call it that if you want, but it seemed a

little rude to me." And that said a lot coming from Serena. She wasn't always known for her tact.

Webster stared at her as if he had no idea what she was talking about. "I was just being a reporter. It's what we do. You have to be direct."

"Maybe that's what you did in New York and then in Washington and then in Richmond. But here in Lantern Beach, we're all kind of a family. You should probably keep that in mind."

Webster stared at her for another moment before offering a curt nod. "Good to know."

Serena sneaked another piece of her crust to Mocha before continuing. "I'll see what I can find out. I'll also see if I can learn anything while I'm on my ice cream patrol."

"Ice cream patrol?" He stared at Serena like she'd lost her mind.

Maybe she had. But she liked it that way.

"I mean, what better person to keep an eye on the neighborhood? I go up and down all of the streets every day. I talk to people around town. And nobody thinks anything about me because I'm the friendly neighborhood ice cream lady. But I can secretly monitor everyone's lives without them thinking a single thing about it."

"Friendly neighborhood ice cream lady? I like that." He slowly nodded as if trying to understand her statement. "Good points . . . I suppose. How about if we regroup tonight after you're done with your route? Would that work?"

"That sounds great. I can come by the newspaper office."

He took another sip of his coffee before nodding. "Perfect. I'll see you then. And by the way, breakfast is on me today."

Serena wouldn't argue with that.

She stood, ready to head home.

She needed to jump on this case.

Especially if she wanted to prove to Ernestine that she was the one for this job instead of Webster.

CHAPTER SEVEN

Serena had just enough time to walk home, pick up her ice cream truck, and start her route. She couldn't start too early because people didn't want to buy ice cream in the morning. Yet, she was surprised at just how many people *did* like to buy ice cream early.

For that reason, she tried to hit all of the streets on the island at least twice during the day, sometimes three times. The later hours were more popular, but the morning wasn't usually a total waste.

She ran her route once. On the second time through, she slowed as she approached the police station. Serena supposed that now was as good a time as any to talk to Cassidy.

She didn't usually feel so nervous before she spoke with Cassidy, but today a touch of dread filled her. She wasn't sure how Cassidy would react to seeing her after Webster's confrontational conversation yesterday.

With Mocha by her side, she stepped into the police station. Paige Henderson, the dispatcher and receptionist, wasn't sitting at the front desk as usual. Instead, Serena went straight toward Cassidy's office. She paused outside the open door and heard the police chief's voice drifting out.

"So you're telling me that there were drugs found in the man's system?" Cassidy said.

Serena's breath caught. Part of her felt like she shouldn't be listening, but the other part couldn't seem to stop. Cassidy must be talking on the phone to someone, probably either Clemson or the state lab.

"Thanks for that information. It's good to know. It seems as if our victim was wrapped up in some unsavory things around town."

It sounded like Cassidy was about to end her call. Before that happened, Serena crept back toward the front door. With any luck, maybe Cassidy wouldn't even know she'd been there. Serena hadn't had to say a word, yet she'd learned so much.

Webster would be pleased. Not that Serena cared what Webster thought. But if he was going to be her editor, then they needed to have a mutual respect for each other. Maybe this would help her earn that.

Armed with her new knowledge, she climbed back into her ice cream truck, grateful that Elsa hadn't decided at that moment to begin playing any music. It would be Serena's luck that the truck would give away her presence at this crucial time.

As she cranked the engine and pulled away, Elsa remained silent. For now, at least.

But Serena was not done investigating yet.

As Serena got closer to the scene of the crime fifteen minutes later, her excitement grew. If there was any place she might find answers, it was here.

First, she hit the road where she'd found Mocha. She scanned everything around her, looking for any kind of clues that she might have missed yesterday.

She saw nothing out of the ordinary.

Mocha, on the other hand, hung his head out the window, his tongue flopping down as if as happy as could be.

Serena smiled.

Did Mocha even miss his owner? The dog just seemed so content with Serena, like they belonged together. It was a little strange, but Serena wasn't complaining. She just wanted to know what this dog's history was.

He was obviously taken care of, well-groomed, and he didn't even have any fleas. She'd noticed that when she gave him a bath last night. She'd also made him rice and gravy, which he'd gobbled up. If he stayed with her longer, she'd need to buy some dog food. Until then, she'd share whatever food she had with her furry friend.

At the end of the lane, Serena turned and made another right. Her next stop was Seashell Lane, the street where the dead body had been found. No one was outside there today.

The next street over had lots of people out, including one family that was grilling. They flagged her down as soon as they saw her, and Serena pulled over.

After she got everybody their treats, she decided to broach the subject of what happened yesterday. The woman at the window seemed chatty, with her sun-kissed cheeks and ponytailed blonde hair.

"I heard about what happened one street over . . ." Serena started.

"I know. We're trying not to let the kids find out about it because we don't want to scare them and ruin their vacation."

"I know. It's so unnerving to think that something would happen like that here in Lantern Beach. But don't worry. It's a fluke. You guys should be safe."

Serena decided not to mention all the other crimes that happened on the island, including a deadly cult that tried to take over and a group of terrorists with an EMP.

And that was just the start.

"Do you know who the man is who passed away?" The woman crossed her arms as she waited for Serena to answer. "Was he a tourist or local?"

"Rumor is that he was from out of town—upstate New York. I saw a picture. He was in his mid-thirties with dark hair, skinny build, and about medium height. He had a Roman nose, and kind of looked like Adrien Brody, the actor. He didn't appear to have been traveling with any family or friends."

The woman drew in a sharp breath and snapped her fingers. "You know, I did see somebody who vaguely matches that description. We're actually nonresident property owners, so we've been here for the past five days. We reserve the house for ourselves for a couple weeks a year."

Maybe Serena was onto something—her first real lead. She couldn't mess up this opportunity. "Where did you see him?"

She pointed toward the entrance of the lane. "Standing at the end of the street. It was late at night, but I had decided to go for a walk on the beach. He was talking to another man. As soon as they saw me, they quieted down."

Serena's heartbeat quickened even more. "Do you have any idea what they were talking about? Did you overhear anything?"

Her lips twisted together in a frown. "It's hard to say, but it did look a little bit heated."

"What about the guy that he was talking to? Was there anything distinct about him?"

The woman tilted her head, obviously trying to think this through. "The only thing distinct that I remember about him was that he had a scar across his cheek. It was dark so it was hard to see much but as he turned his face, the full moon hit. That's when I saw the scar."

"What kind of scar exactly?"

"It was almost like he had a cut right across his left cheek at one time."

As soon as she said the words, Serena knew exactly who she was talking about.

Carl Linton.

That was the second mention of the man.

He was the island dogcatcher, and Serena needed to talk to him ASAP.

CHAPTER EIGHT

Serena thanked the woman for her help before continuing down the street.

Finally, she had a suspect—a vague one, but that was okay. Serena could flesh this out more. What if their local dogcatcher was also dealing drugs?

He didn't seem like the type. Then again, maybe that would make him the perfect one to be involved in an illegal activity like that.

As she reached the end of the lane and pulled into a driveway to turn around, Mocha began to growl.

She glanced around and saw nothing except some woods and another vacation house.

What could Mocha be growling about? It didn't make sense.

Maybe he'd just caught a whiff of another dog in the area. Didn't dogs do that? They got all territorial when they smelled another animal in their space, right? From Serena's recollection, that seemed correct.

It didn't matter. Right now, Serena had learned something valuable. She had a suspect.

The dogcatcher.

She glanced back over at Mocha again and frowned. But if the dogcatcher was somehow involved, did that mean that Mocha was also somehow involved? That thought didn't sit well with her. She already felt protective of the little furball.

She needed to talk to Carl. It wasn't unusual to see the man driving around town looking for stray animals while Serena was on her route. Could she even hope to be as lucky today to run across him? Could she somehow use this dogcatcher outfit to her advantage? How exactly could she find out what this man had been up to lately?

She let the questions turn over in her head for a few minutes. Did she and Carl have any of the same connections? On an island of this size, it seemed certain that they would. Serena just had to figure out what those links were.

That's when she realized that Kai actually had a connection to the family. Kai was friends with Carl's wife, Janine. But would Kai open up to her again? Maybe for another free Bomb Pop?

It was worth a try. Especially if it meant justice for the dead man . . . and if it meant keeping precious little Mocha safe.

As Serena headed out of this area, she bypassed several streets she'd normally hit. She was practically salivating as she tried to find answers to this murder. If she was honest with herself, she might even admit that part of her wanted to find answers before Webster did.

Which was ridiculous.

This wasn't a competition—this was an investigation for an article. Someone had died, so there were no games involved here. Yet that didn't stop the urgency she felt inside.

She needed to talk to someone—someone who might have some answers for her.

Kai.

Serena knew the woman wouldn't be cleaning today. She only did that on the weekends in-between guests at the vacation homes. During the week, she actually worked at Serena's aunt's fruit and vegetable stand.

That's where Serena headed.

She pulled up to the The Happy Hippie and

parked. The converted vintage Chevy van was located in the corner of a parking lot by a bait and tackle store. It had been painted a bright turquoise, and one side had been removed to make room for a makeshift wood pergola. Under the wooden arms were rows of baskets filled with local produce.

The line was three people deep with customers waiting to pay, each holding bamboo baskets filled with fresh food. Skye was behind the checkout counter as well as Kai.

Her aunt looked up and smiled as Serena approached, placing a cantaloupe from the basket on the counter to ring it up. "Hey, Serena. What brings you by?"

"Can't a girl just stop by to chat?"

"You can. You just don't usually." Skye continued unloading more produce, some tomatoes and cucumbers this time. Her gaze traveled down to Mocha. "Who is this? Certainly, you didn't adopt a dog just to use him as a prop for your dogcatcher persona?"

"No," she snorted. "Of course not. I'm . . . dog-sitting until his owner is found."

Mocha wagged his tail until Skye tossed a carrot down to him. The dog ate it up, acting like it tasted just as good as a bone.

"Is everything okay?" Skye continued.

"I actually have a question for Kai once she's free."

Kai's eyes widened with a touch of amusement. "But you asked me your questions last night. Second time, my costs will be a double. A Bomb Pop and a screwball."

"It's a deal."

Kai paused from restocking some jars of homemade firecracker pickles, almost looking surprised. "Aren't you just an inquisitive girl?"

Skye looked over at Kai. "Believe me, yes, she is. Go ahead. Take a little break. I'll be fine here, and I'll call you if it gets too busy."

"Thanks, Skye," Serena called.

She and Kai stepped behind the fruit stand and swatted away some flies that buzzed near the discarded produce pile.

"So, what's going on now?" Kai crossed her arms but seemed unable to stay still. As she glanced down, something seemed to catch her eye, and she began pulling some weeds from the cracks in the asphalt.

"I know my questions might sound a little crazy, but there's this new editor in town at the newspaper. He's taking the job that I should have had. I need to find answers in this investigation before he does if I want to prove myself."

"You should totally have that job." She tossed a

clump of grass into the sand behind them. "You've worked hard for it."

Serena nodded. "I know, right?"

"So what do you need to know?"

"Are you friends with Janine Linton?"

"Carl's wife?"

"The one and only."

She shrugged and grabbed some more weeds. "I don't know if I'd say we're friends, but we do play bunco together once a week. Why? What do you need to know?"

"Carl's name has come up a couple times in this investigation, and I'm wondering if he might somehow be involved. Do you know him very well?"

"Carl? No, I hardly know him at all. Like I said, I only know Janine through bunco."

"Does Janine ever say anything about Carl?"

Kai straightened and shrugged. "As a matter of fact, she has mentioned him a few times. She said he's seemed preoccupied lately, especially ever since he got the high cholesterol diagnosis. I don't want to make anyone look guilty who's innocent, but I've personally wondered if the man is seeing someone else. Janine says he disappears for hours at a time and looks guilty when he gets home. Maybe it's one of those midlife crisis things. I never got married just so I could avoid drama like this."

Serena's breath caught. Could Carl be disappearing for hours at a time, not because he was seeing someone else, but because he was involved with something illegal? It seemed like a good guess, one that deserved a follow-up.

Serena thanked Kai and then went back to her ice cream truck with Mocha trotting beside her.

She was going to do her ice cream route one more time, and then she was going to focus all her energy on Carl.

CHAPTER NINE

Just as Serena was finishing up her route for the day, she spotted a familiar truck in the distance.

Carl's animal control vehicle.

He pulled into the parking lot near the boardwalk area.

Could this be it? Was Carl going to meet a mystery woman? Or maybe he was going to meet a colleague so he could somehow pass drugs between them.

Serena didn't know, but there was no time like the present to find out.

She pulled into the same parking lot and waited until Carl had exited his vehicle. Then she climbed out herself, trying to keep an eye on the man.

She was going to need to be sneaky here, and

dressing like a dogcatcher today maybe hadn't been the best idea. But, if Serena remembered later, she would come back and try to take a selfie with his animal control vehicle. Her social media friends would love that.

But that was for another time.

"Mocha, you stay close," she told the dog. The last thing she needed was for Carl to try to snatch her dog.

Not *her* dog, she corrected herself again. But this new dog that she was temporarily taking care of.

Just the thought of that made a sprig of sadness grow in her.

It had been nice having someone other than herself to talk to. Plus, Mocha got a lot of attention. Children had loved petting him, and Mocha had soaked up the affection. He was pretty much the perfect dog.

Serena watched as Carl went to the hostess desk at The Docks. The seafood restaurant had an outdoor patio and an indoor porch area. Whenever Serena had been here, the placed had smelled like Old Bay and saltwater. The combination was actually pretty great.

The woman at the hostess stand led Carl inside to be seated.

Now Serena somehow needed to get close enough to figure out what he was doing.

"How are we going to do this, Mocha?" She glanced down at the dog, who stood beside her, waiting for further instructions.

It had been one thing to sneak the dog into The Crazy Chefette. Serena knew Lisa well enough to know her friend would forgive her if the dog was caught inside. But Serena didn't know the owner of The Docks, and she didn't think the man would take kindly to having an animal inside his restaurant. Serena had met the man once or twice, and he had a very strong personality, to say the least.

Serena glanced around again. At one of the nearby shops she saw an assortment of baby slings for sale. An idea began to form in her mind. Would this really work?

It seemed worth a try.

She slipped inside the store and grabbed the cheapest sling she could find. After paying, she escaped into the bathroom and wrapped it over her chest. She lifted Mocha and put the dog snug inside the fabric there.

She glanced in the mirror. If someone didn't look closely, this might actually work—if Mocha cooperated, of course.

Right now, the dog was being very compliant. He

simply lay there like a little baby and, as long as Serena rubbed his tummy, he seemed pretty content.

She hoped this would work, for a minute, at least.

Drawing in a deep breath, she exited the store and headed toward The Docks. Thankfully, it was in between lunch and dinner so the place wasn't packed yet. Come dinnertime, there would probably be a wait time of at least an hour. This was one of the reasons Serena tried not to eat out too much during the tourist season. Everything was always so packed.

She plastered on her best smile as she approached the hostess. Serena didn't recognize the woman. The teenager had been brought in as summer help, most likely.

"Hi, I'd like a table for one inside," Serena said, bouncing on her feet and rubbing the baby sling to keep Mocha quiet.

The woman glanced at Serena's midsection and smiled. "Of course. You gotta get that baby out of the sun, huh?"

Serena smiled and nodded, trying to act like this was all normal.

A moment later, she was seated inside the restaurant. Dark paneling covered the walls, and the whole place had a cave-like atmosphere, despite the screened-in windows all around them.

But, across the way, sat Carl Linton. He was in the

corner, about five tables away. His back was turned to the rest of the restaurant. But Serena could see enough.

She saw a napkin had been spread open and stuffed into his shirt. Could see his thick back and the crown of dark hair around his head.

No one else sat with him, but that didn't mean that somebody else wasn't coming. Serena glanced at the menu, trying to look natural. As she did, Mocha wiggled.

No doubt the scent of food had alerted him to where they were.

She tried to gently rub his stomach to keep him calm, but the wiggles were still there.

She was going to have to act quickly before she created a scene. She smiled at the waitress as a glass of water was set in front of her.

"Do you need a few minutes or do you know what you want to order?" the woman asked.

"I'm going to need a minute," Serena said. "In fact, I'm going to run to the restroom real quick."

Mocha wiggled again and all kinds of bad scenarios played out in Serena's mind.

Instead of going to the restroom, Serena bypassed that area and walked straight over to Carl. She was just going to need to confront him right here.

She slid into one of the empty chairs across from him. When he saw her, his eyes widened.

"Can I help you?" Carl asked, pausing mid-bite.

Serena got right to the point. "What are you up to?"

His face went a little pale. "I don't know what you're talking about."

"What do you know about the dead man whose body was found on the island yesterday?"

His eyes grew even wider. "I don't know anything about the dead man. What are you getting at?"

"I know you're hiding something. I know you were talking to the dead man a couple days before he died. For that matter, everyone in town knows that you've been hiding something. Maybe even something criminal."

Mocha wiggled, and Serena rubbed his tummy even more. Still, the dog let out a little whine.

Carl's eyes narrowed in confusion as he looked at the baby wrap.

She needed to divert his attention. Quickly.

"What are you hiding, Carl?" she repeated.

Sweat sprinkled across his forehead as he shifted his attention back to her. "I'm not hiding anything."

"Look." Serena leaned closer. "I'm giving you the benefit of the doubt. I came here to talk to you myself instead of going to the police. But that will be my next step if you don't come clean with me."

He set his fork and knife down, and his words came out quickly as he said, "I'm not doing anything illegal, if that's what you're getting at."

Then what else could he possibly be doing? Serena narrowed her eyes. "I'm not so sure I believe that. What's with all the sneakiness? Need I remind you that you were seen riding around the very area where the dead man was found."

"That's because I'm a dogcatcher!" His voice rose until a couple people glanced his way.

Serena wasn't ready to back down yet. "But you don't usually just cruise the streets now, do you?"

"There were reports of some dogs barking, and it was disturbing the neighbors." His words stumbled into each other. "I went to check it out, but I didn't find anything. Are you happy now?"

No, as a matter of fact, she wasn't. "What about that man you were talking to? The one that ended up dead? Paul Witherspoon was his name."

"He was one of the people that called to report the barking. There's nothing illegal about talking to someone who wanted to file a report. I was doing my job."

Carl was right. He could have been doing his job. But that didn't mean he was innocent either.

Serena leaned closer, ready to seal this deal and prove he was guilty. Then she could write this article and rightfully take the job she was meant for.

"It doesn't explain your sneakiness," she continued.

He let out a long sigh. "I don't know how many times I can say this. You're barking up the wrong tree."

"Are you sure you're not involved in smuggling drugs?"

"Drugs?" He repeated a little too loudly. "Are you off your rocker?"

"I still don't think you're telling me the whole story, Carl."

He rubbed a hand over his face. "Okay, I am hiding something. Are you happy now?"

Excitement buzzed through her. "That depends. Are you going to tell me what you're hiding?"

He looked down at his plate. "I'm supposed to be watching my diet and only eating rabbit food. But I can't bring myself to do that. So I come here on occasion and I order some fried fish, french fries, and coleslaw. The whole cholesterol-laden shebang."

She glanced at his plate and realized he was telling the truth. The only thing he was hiding was his bad diet habits. It looked like her so-called lead had totally fizzled.

"I see," Serena finally said. "Good talk."

He narrowed his eyes at her.

Just then, Mocha wiggled again. Before Serena could stop the dog, he sprang from the baby carrier and jumped on the table.

He began to gobble up Carl's cholesterol-laden food.

People at the tables around them gasped and stared. A waitress charged their way. Carl jumped to his feet, his chair falling behind him and drawing even more attention to the scene.

Serena frowned and she tried to pull Mocha away.

It looked like Carl wasn't going to get to cheat on his new relationship with healthy food. Not today, at least.

Serena left the restaurant. After many apologies and paying for Carl's food, she and Mocha made their way back to her ice cream truck. She had just enough time to meet Webster.

As if right on cue, her phone rang. It was Webster.

"Listen, I was wondering if instead of coming into the office we could meet at the pier?"

"The festivities there aren't until Tuesday night," she reminded him.

"That's okay. I just want to get out of the office for a while. It seems more relaxing to talk on the beach than it does here at my aunt's house."

Serena had to wonder if there was some tension between Ernestine and Webster. Either way, the beach was always preferred over being inside. "That sounds good. I can meet you in fifteen minutes."

He agreed, and, right on time, Serena pulled into the parking lot by the pier. As soon as she stepped outside, the sound of the ocean hit her, as did the scent of sea air. Somewhere in the distance, someone played acoustic music, maybe on a radio. Put it all together, and a moment of bliss filled her.

Times like this were what made her love this area.

As she walked with Mocha to meet Webster, she glanced around. Numerous fishermen were on the pier, their lines strung into the water. Several people had already stretched their hammocks beneath the massive wooden structure, and a bonfire blazed not far away. This was a favorite spot, especially for locals.

Serena spotted Webster. He still wore his stuffy, city boy outfit. He'd set up two beach chairs facing the ocean and waved her over.

"We can do this, Mocha," Serena muttered.

"We're not going to let him drive us crazy. Nor are we going to let him get the upper hand. We will be victorious."

"Hey, there," Webster greeted her. "How's it going?"

Serena considered exactly how much she wanted to share with him. She decided to leave off the little incident that had just happened at the restaurant and stick with the facts—the very vague facts. "It's going."

"I have something for you." He handed her a gift bag.

"For me?" Was this some kind of trick? Maybe a nameplate that read: Serena Lavinia, Not the Editor-in-Chief. Or Serena Lavinia, Underling?

Webster nodded. "Open it."

She shoved the tissue paper aside and saw . . . a dog leash and collar inside.

It wasn't just any dog leash—this one had cheerful emojis up and down the length of it, each one reminding Serena of her ever-changing looks. "This is great. Thank you."

"I thought you might need it." He shrugged, like it wasn't a big deal.

"I'm sure we'll get a lot of use out of this." After slipping the collar and leash onto Mocha, she turned toward Webster. "And, by the way, in addition to helping you with this article about the dead man, I would like to do an article on the beach art being left around town."

His eyebrows shot up. "You mean like the heart we saw yesterday?"

"That's right. Today somebody left a smiling sun. I really want to figure out who's behind this. Of course, our first priority is finding out information about this man who was murdered. But I thought the art could be a good human-interest piece."

"Of course." Webster pushed his glasses up again. "I think it's a good idea to do a story on this. People always like feel-good pieces along with the hard-hitting news."

Good. She could check that off her list. Now onto her next item. "That said, I do have a few updates on our investigation into the dead man."

"Me too," Webster said. "You go first."

Somehow, Serena felt like this was a trick, but she decided to comply anyway. "I was able to learn from the police chief that there was some type of drug found in Paul Witherspoon's system."

His eyebrows shot up. "Is that right? Very interesting."

"I thought so too. So maybe all of this has to do with drugs. It's not unusual for people to try to smuggle items off these shores. It's been done before.

The seclusion of Lantern Beach seems to beckon all types of illegal activities here on the coast."

"Noted. Anything else?"

"And I had one lead but it fizzled. The dogcatcher's name had come up a few times, but it turns out the only thing he's doing wrong might put him in a hospital instead of jail. He's supposed to be watching what he eats, but he's unable to give up his fried foods. It was a bit of a letdown."

"It sounds like you've done good work today, Serena. Thanks for all the time you put in."

"What about you?" She was anxious to hear what he may have learned.

He wiped some sand from his leg before turning toward her, his eyes lit with a secret he was on the cusp of sharing. "I was able to find out a couple things today. Starting with the fact that the family who'd been staying in the yellow house claims they have no idea who Paul Witherspoon is."

"Good to know."

"I also found somebody today who lives on the street where our dead man was found. He had some pretty interesting footage that was caught on his video doorbell."

Serena sat up straighter. It sounded like an excellent lead. "Do you have the footage?"

"As a matter of fact, they did share it with me."

Webster pulled out his phone and hit a few buttons. A moment later, a video appeared on the screen.

Serena watched closely as two figures ran across the screen. "Can you play that again?" She wished there was a slow-motion option so she could soak in all the details better.

"Of course." Webster hit a button, and it began to play again.

This time she got a better look. That was definitely their dead guy who was running. Another man chased him. The images were too blurry for Serena to pick up any particulars about the man, only that he wore a hat and sweatshirt.

"One more time?" she asked.

Webster complied.

When she watched the video this time, she noticed one new detail. "Mocha . . ."

The dead man had been chasing Mocha.

Just how was her dog involved in all of this?

She rubbed Mocha's head. She didn't know. And she didn't like it.

CHAPTER TEN

"This means that Mocha was somehow involved in that man's death." The words left Serena's lips in rapid fire.

"It at least means that the dead man had something to do with Mocha," Webster said. "But I guess you already knew that, right? I mean, why else would the dog have had Paul Witherspoon's shoe in his mouth?"

Serena frowned and rubbed the dog's head. "I hoped it was just a fluke or something."

"But in order for the dog to have the shoe, that means Sprinkles—I mean, Mocha—must have been in the enclosed fenced-in area. Was the gate closed when you found the dead man?"

Serena replayed the day. "It was. But Mocha's legs

are pretty springy. He can easily jump over things so I just assumed he jumped in and out."

"So let's lay out what we know so far." Webster shifted toward her. "I want to go over these things with you before I run the article tomorrow morning. We know that drugs were most likely involved in Paul Witherspoon's death. He was stabbed and either pushed or fell into the pool. Nobody on the island has come forward to say that they were here with him or know him. We don't know where he was staying yet either. But now we have this footage that confirms that somebody—most likely the killer—was chasing him before he died."

A chill washed over her. "It looks like we have footage of the killer himself, doesn't it?" Serena thought that would make her feel better but it didn't. Instead, somehow she felt more uneasy.

"The question is, what do you get when you put all of that together? You've ruled out the dogcatcher. Good job." He fired at her with a finger gun. "But who else could this be? What could be going on?"

"Well, if drugs were involved and Mocha is involved . . ." Her thoughts drifted. "What if they were using Mocha as a drug mule?"

"That seems highly unlikely," Webster said.

As soon as the words left her lips, she had realized how ridiculous they sounded. But did her theory have any validity? She was at least thankful that Webster hadn't laughed at her.

But when she didn't say anything for a few minutes, he did say, "Has Mocha shown any signs of discomfort?"

Serena rubbed Mocha's head. "No."

"Then I really think we need to think on a slightly smaller scale than that."

He was probably right. "Why would someone be chasing sweet little Mocha then?"

"It could be as simple as the fact that Mocha belonged to our victim. Maybe Mocha got out of the house, our victim chased him, and the killer just happened to see it happen and used that opportunity to strike."

"But that still doesn't tell us why this guy could have died. We need motive."

Webster frowned. "That's why we need to keep investigating."

Serena let out a long breath. "What are you thinking now? Do you have any other theories?"

"Not yet. But I'm still working on it. I'm not ready to give up yet."

Just as he said those words, Serena felt a shadow fall over her. She turned in time to see Cassidy walking toward her with a man Serena had never seen before. Serena quickly observed the stranger. He was probably in his forties, about thirty pounds overweight, and his thick brows shadowed his eyes.

"I was hoping I might find you." Cassidy stopped in front of them.

"How did you find me?" Serena asked. Maybe it wasn't the best first question, but it had slipped out.

"Your ice cream truck's a little hard to miss," she said. "Serena, Webster. This is Jason. He came into the police station because his dog was lost. It turns out his dog is Sprinkles."

"You mean, Mocha," Serena corrected.

Cassidy squinted. "What? Never mind. Either way, you'll be happy to know that the dog can now safely return home."

Panic rush through Serena. She looked down at Mocha and noticed that her little dog had gone tense. Just as Jason reached for the canine, Mocha let out a growl. The man withdrew his hand.

"Are you sure this is his dog?" Serena asked, her gaze on Cassidy.

"He showed me some of the vet bills," Cassidy said. "This is definitely his dog."

Serena held on to the leash.

"Serena," Cassidy said, a warning in her voice. "You have to give the dog back."

"But Mocha doesn't want to go," Serena said, literally digging in her heels.

Cassidy turned toward Jason. "Is there a reason your dog doesn't seem to like you?"

"This dog's always been temperamental." He shrugged. "Come on, Bob. We need to get you home. Mom is going to be happy to see you. She's missed you a lot."

Mocha continued to growl low and steady.

And who would name a dog like Mocha something boring like Bob?

"Serena, give him the leash," Cassidy said, warning in her voice.

If there was one thing Serena knew, it was that she was not giving this dog back to this man. Not if she could help it.

"Fine," she muttered. But as she let go of the leash, she leaned toward Mocha. "Run, boy! Run!"

As if Mocha understood, the dog raced in the opposite direction, away from his so-called owner.

Cassidy and Jason took off after Mocha, but the dog was too fast. By the time the canine disappeared into the woods near the end of the beach, they were both too far behind to catch him.

Satisfaction stretched through Serena, but she tried not to smile.

Cassidy and Jason stomped through the sand back toward Serena and Webster. Cassidy was on the phone, probably calling Carl at animal control to let him know to be on the lookout. And she looked none too happy as her gaze went to Serena.

"That was a bold move," Webster whispered.

"I don't know what the connection is between that man and Mocha, but that dog doesn't want anything to do with his supposed owner. There was no way I could let Mocha go, considering the situation."

"I don't blame you."

Surprise washed through Serena. She'd fully expected a lecture from him, and, instead, Webster looked impressed. He scored a few points with her for that.

But the good feelings only lasted a moment as Cassidy and Jason joined them. Jason drew in deep, ragged breaths, almost as if he hadn't gotten that much exercise in years.

"That wasn't your smartest move, Serena." Cassidy narrowed her eyes.

"If he really is this dog's supposed owner, then Mocha would have run to him, right? I can't control what that dog does. I've only known the dog for one day. Why would he listen to me?"

Cassidy's narrowed gaze still remained on

Serena. Regardless of Cassidy's professional stare, she couldn't help but to think that Cassidy would've done the same thing. But she also knew that Cassidy probably couldn't say that in front of Jason.

That's what she wanted to believe, at least.

"You're going to pay for this," Jason said, his nostrils flaring.

"Was that a threat?" Cassidy rolled her shoulders back and turned toward "Bob's" owner.

"No, it wasn't a threat, but you should be arresting her." His arm shot out and he pointed at Serena.

"Lawfully speaking, she didn't do anything wrong," Cassidy said. "It could be argued that it wasn't nice, but there's nothing illegal about not being kind."

Jason continued to glower at Serena. "You better hope nothing happens to that dog."

Cassidy took his arm. "We're going to find your dog, sir. Now you need to calm down."

As Cassidy led him away, she passed one more glance back at Serena.

Serena shrugged. She wasn't going to apologize for what she'd done, and nothing was going to change her mind about that.

"That guy really wants Mocha," Webster said.

"I know. And that makes me very suspicious. I've gotta find Mocha before he does."

Webster stood. "I'll go with you."

Serena glanced at Webster one more time, unsure if she'd heard him correctly.

She had.

Maybe this guy wasn't as bad as she thought. Not if he was willing to look for a lost dog.

CHAPTER ELEVEN

Webster and Serena drove around for two hours looking for Mocha, but they had no luck finding the dog. With every minute that passed, Serena's worry grew. What if the dog was lost? Hurt? What if Carl found Mocha before they did? Or, even worse, what if Jason had somehow been able to locate the dog?

She began to question her decision to let the dog go. Though she initially felt like the dog would be safer anywhere but with Jason, now it seemed like a bad idea. Mocha could be lost and alone out there, not to mention scared.

Webster glanced over at her as he pulled over onto the side of the road near the woods where Mocha had disappeared. They'd taken his sedan on the hunt, which was a good thing. Serena's hands trembled with nerves.

"We'll find him," Webster told her.

"I'll never forgive myself if something happens to that dog and it was my fault."

"You were just trying to protect the dog."

"But what if I made the wrong choice?" Her throat burned as she said the words.

"Sometimes you can only make the best choice that you know to make at the time."

Something about the way Webster said the words made Serena think that he'd had some firsthand experience with that. But she didn't ask any questions. If Webster wanted to share something with her then he would.

"I guess I should probably get back to my house." Serena glanced over at him, hating to admit defeat. But she had no idea where else to look for her dog.

Or . . . *that* dog, she should say. Mocha wasn't hers. But Mocha felt like he *should* be hers.

"I'll drop you off at your ice cream truck then. I should probably get back too so I can work on this article. I want to post an update on the case."

"I wish you had more of an update to post," Serena said.

"Me too. But the answers will come. Eventually."

He pulled up beside Elsa and put his vehicle into

Park. Serena's hand went to the door, and she started to open it but paused. "Thank you again for your help. I appreciate it."

"It's no problem." He flashed a smile that almost made him look handsome. His eyes crinkled at the sides, the rigid set of his shoulders softened, and even his breathing seemed to even. "Stay safe, okay?"

She nodded, her heart lodging in her throat. "I will. You too."

Back at her house, Serena lay in her hammock, staring up at the stars and wishing they had the answers about sweet little Mocha. But the answers felt just as elusive as what was out there beyond the great unknown.

Worry squeezed her insides. She closed her eyes and prayed that Mocha was okay. She was tempted to go back out and look for the dog more, yet she feared that the dark road would be a foe instead of a friend. Maybe her best bet would just be to look again in the morning.

The one thing that she knew for sure was that that dog was somehow mixed up in this murder. She couldn't figure out the connection. Not yet. But something was going on.

She kept replaying that footage from the video doorbell. Who could the man chasing their victim be? Jason?

She nibbled on her lip as she thought about it. She supposed the men were approximately the same size. But it was almost impossible to know for sure, especially considering that the man in the video had been wearing a hat and oversized clothing.

They really had to tell Cassidy about that video. In fact, Serena probably should have told Cassidy the information earlier. But Serena was so angry at the prospect of giving up Mocha that she hadn't been thinking clearly.

Granted, Serena wasn't the one who officially had a copy of that video. Webster did. How was he going to feel about turning that information over to the police?

Serena still couldn't figure that man out yet. One minute, he seemed bossy and imposing. The next, he seemed thoughtful and kind.

Men . . .

She swung back and forth on the hammock, her thoughts swaying along with her.

Mocha . . . how had that dog wormed his way into her heart so quickly? It made no sense. She never even thought of herself as a dog person. Something about Mocha had seemed different. He had been a great companion for the past day and a half.

Tomorrow was a new day. Maybe Serena could find more answers. But her first priority was going to be finding Mocha.

She let her hand fall to the side of the hammock as she lay there. And as it did, her fingers brushed something soft.

Her heart raced.

She sat up in the hammock and looked down, hardly able to breathe. She sucked in a breath at what she saw.

"Mocha?"

The dog barked, and Serena scooped him into her arms. He rewarded her with doggy kisses.

"You came back," she murmured. She held the little furball to her chest, his scent—now mixed with the woodsy outdoors—filling her with comfort.

Now she had to figure out how to protect him.

CHAPTER TWELVE

The next morning, Serena put on a Dorothy from the Wizard of Oz outfit. She had side braids, along with a blue and white checked dress. She added some red lipstick and some penny loafers, and she was ready to go.

Except that she didn't know exactly what to do with Nutty Buddy today. Yes, Nutty Buddy. She'd decided that was a better name for the canine.

For today, at least.

She couldn't leave the dog home by himself. Yet it also felt dangerous to take him out.

After contemplating her options for a few minutes, Serena finally decided to drive with the dog down to the beach. They could both stretch their legs and get a little serenity for the day. Usually there were very few people out at this hour anyway. Plus,

Serena wanted to check and see if there was any new beach art.

As soon as she stepped outside, she saw something on her deck. Was that . . . a piece of steak?

Her shoulder muscles tightened.

Her gaze continued to the sandy grass leading to the lane.

A trail of steak chunks had been left there!

She grabbed Nutty Buddy's leash and held him back. "You don't want to do that, boy."

A bad feeling brewed in her stomach.

Cautiously, she skirted around the steak and walked toward the lane. As she reached it, she peered around a lattice wall there.

As she did, a black car pulled away.

Someone had been trying to lure Nutty Buddy away. They'd laid breadcrumbs—er, steak crumbs—to lead the canine to their vehicle.

Her heart pounded in her chest at the thought. That was despicable. She was so glad Webster had gotten her this leash. Otherwise . . .

She leaned down and hugged Nutty Buddy. The dog licked her in return.

Serena was cautious as she walked Nutty Buddy at

the beach. Her gaze continually scanned everything around her. She didn't see anyone else.

As soon as she saw the beach art, she felt better. Today, the artist had created what looked like waves.

Just as before, everything was arranged perfectly, from the colors and shapes of the shells to the design itself. Whoever had done this was really talented. She pulled out her phone and took a picture.

After Nutty Buddy had done his business and Serena had cleaned up after him, she went back to the ice cream truck. She glanced around, making sure that nobody was watching or trying to lure Nutty Buddy away.

She saw no one.

As soon as she reached her truck, her phone rang. It was Webster.

"Hey, I know this is unconventional, but I was wondering if you could pick me up?" he said.

She shoved her eyebrows together in confusion. "I'm doing my normal ice cream route today . . ."

"I know. I have my laptop. I can work some as you drive. You'll hardly know I'm there."

This entire conversation seemed suspicious. "Are you sure you want to do that?"

"Yeah, I'm sure. There are some things I want to talk to you about, and I figured this would be the best way to do it."

"But I thought I wouldn't know you were there," she said.

"I said hardly. That word was very important to that sentence."

He had a point. "Okay then. I'll swing by Ernestine's house in about ten minutes."

"Sounds like a plan."

Serena climbed into her truck, feeling a strange sense of curiosity. Why in the world did Webster want to ride with her? Was it really so they could talk?

If that was the truth, then she supposed she could appreciate that he wasn't interrupting her schedule in order to talk about the newspaper. Speaking of which . . .

She pulled out her phone and pulled up the newspaper's website. There at the very top was an article about their dead man.

Her eyes widened when she saw the byline.

Webster had included her name.

That was nice, at least. Serena had halfway expected him to take all the credit himself. Maybe she shouldn't be so hard on the man. But she wasn't ready to trust him yet either.

A few minutes later, she pulled up in front of Ernestine's house and Webster hopped into the ice cream truck. As he did, his eyes widened.

"Mocha?" He glanced up at Serena as he rubbed the dog's head.

"It's Nutty Buddy."

"But—" He froze and then shook his head. "Never mind."

Serena shrugged. "He showed up at my place last night."

"Did you tell the police chief?"

"No, not yet. I don't know what I should do. I don't want to break the law, but I'm not giving this dog back."

His eyes widened. "So you're just going to keep him hidden for now?"

"I don't know what else to do." She told him about the steak trail she'd found outside her place this morning. "What would you do in this situation?"

She halfway expected Webster to give a noble answer. Like turning the dog in no matter the cost. Instead he said, "I would do the same thing. Someone's obviously desperate to get this dog. That doesn't settle well with me."

Something warm and fuzzy started to grow down deep inside her. "So you really just want to ride around with me today?"

"I thought it would just be a good way for us to talk. If this case does have something to do with Sprinkles—I mean, Mocha—I mean, Nutty Buddy."

He shook his head. "Then I know you're going to want to find answers sooner rather than later."

"Something did occur to me last night," Serena said. "I'm not sure if it means anything, but . . ."

"There are no bad ideas when you're brainstorming. That's what my old editor used to always tell me."

She sucked in a breath. "Okay then. When I was talking to Carl, the dogcatcher, he said that somebody had reported a lot of dogs barking at night in the area where our dead man was found. I'm wondering if that's somehow related?"

"I suppose it's worth considering. Where do you think we should start?"

"I want to go back to that street where our victim was found. Whatever is happening, that area is Ground Zero."

"I think that's a good idea," Webster said.

Serena shouldn't feel as pleased as she did, but she couldn't stop herself. Maybe she liked approval more than she thought.

However, she couldn't simply dive into this. She did have other commitments that needed to be met. "First, I need to do at least part of my route. I have patrons counting on me."

"Of course," Webster said. "I'm along for the ride, friendly neighborhood ice cream lady.

Speaking of which, do you have any chocolate fudge bars?"

"I do. I always say you can judge a person by the kind of ice cream they order."

His eyebrows shot up. "And what does the fudge pop say about me?"

"That you're classic, responsible, and you like routine."

"What if I'd gotten a Bomb Pop?"

"That would mean you like excitement and you're the life of the party."

Webster crossed his arms and turned toward Serena. "And what kind of ice cream would you get?"

"Easy. A screwball. I'm sweet and messy, but there's a gumball as a reward at the end of it all."

She flashed a smile as Webster's chuckle filled the truck.

She liked that sound . . . a little more than she should.

Serena felt the anticipation grow in her as she reached the street that she was now calling Ground Zero. As she passed Lawrence's house, the man stepped outside and flagged them down. The sound of Elsa playing "Polly, Put the Kettle On" was obviously irresistible.

Good. He was just the person she was hoping to run into.

"How's business going?" He leaned in the window.

Serena shoved Nutty Buddy behind her so nobody would see the dog.

Webster leaned across the seat, his arm blocking the canine from coming up.

"Business as usual." Serena tried to keep her voice casual. "How's your vacation going?"

"I can't complain. Now that all the excitement across the street is over, I've been back to surfing every day. Seems a bit like a shame to be having a good time while other people have suffered. But . . ." He shrugged.

"So everything's been quiet on the street ever since then, huh?" Serena asked.

"Yeah, I guess you could say that. I'm not complaining."

Was this man hiding something? He always seemed to be in the middle of everything. But Serena had nothing to prove that he might be involved.

A few minutes later, she served him a chocolate chip ice cream cookie sandwich and continued down to the end of the street.

Just as before, as they reached the patch of woods, Nutty Buddy began to growl.

Serena and Webster glanced at each other. Last time, Serena had written this off as just a coincidence.

But what if it wasn't? Same place, same reaction.

Besides that, this was the same area that Carl said someone called him about when they'd heard dogs barking.

"What's through there?" Webster asked, pointing toward a stretch of trees.

"I thought it was just woods."

He turned toward her, an unrestrained curiosity in his eyes. "What do you think? Maybe we should find out."

"You think that whatever is back there holds the answers to all of this?"

"I'd say it's worth a try. But if things turn ugly, we call the police."

Instead of turning around in the driveway, she kept going toward the dead end. As she reached it, she saw a narrow path there. It was just wide enough for a vehicle to pass through.

She stared hard. "There's a house back there," she whispered.

"You didn't know it was there?" Webster asked, staring at the rundown structure.

"I had no idea. You can't hardly even see the road back here, and I've been this way plenty of times."

Just then Nutty Buddy growled again.

What did that dog know that they didn't?

"I think we should leave the ice cream truck here and approach by foot. What do you think?" Serena asked.

"I think that's a good idea," Webster said.

Serena had to admit that she felt a touch of hesitation as she climbed from Elsa. She took Nutty Buddy's leash, just to be safe. But the dog was still on guard. There was something about this property that he didn't like.

They stayed on the edge of the lane as they approach the house. But as they got closer, she heard the sound of dogs barking. More than one dog barking, for sure. There had to be at least five or six.

Serena and Webster exchanged glances with each other. What was going on here?

They continued through the woods, despite the underbrush. Serena reached down and lifted Nutty Buddy in her arms so he wouldn't get caught in any of the thistles.

The house in the distance was surrounded by water, with a long dock stretching from the bulkhead. She spotted a decent-sized boat at the end of the wooden walkway and a man hurried toward the watercraft with something in his hands.

Was that a . . . cage? Her breath caught. It was!

A picture started to form in her head, but she didn't like the images that came together. She needed more information first.

They continued to watch. The man went back and forth on the boat and loaded at least six different cages. As he did, the barking became louder. There were clearly animals in those cages.

"It's a dog-smuggling ring," Webster said.

That's exactly what Serena had been thinking. But she wanted to hear more of his opinion first. She didn't know much about these types of things and maybe thought they only existed in fiction.

"Tell me more," she said.

"I covered something like this when I was in New York. People steal high-end dogs and then sell them to families who are willing to pay thousands of dollars for these dogs."

"Aren't they microchipped?"

"I'm sure there are ways to either take the microchip out or somehow wipe it clean without removing it."

"But why would they be doing this on Lantern Beach?"

"My guess is that this is the easiest way to transport these dogs up and down the coast. People probably aren't going to be paying too much attention to a boat. But if they're on the highway and they stop to get gas? If people hear dogs barking, they're going to get suspicious."

Serena held Nutty Buddy closer. This boy must've been a part of this mess, but he'd somehow gotten away. And, for some reason, Paul Witherspoon must've died because of all this.

She squinted as she saw the man on the dock walking back toward the house. It was Jason!

She had had no doubt that man was involved in this operation. From the moment she met him, he had given her a bad feeling. And rightfully so.

"We've got to do something to stop this," Serena whispered.

Webster pulled out his phone. "Let's start by calling Chief Chambers."

"Good idea."

As he dialed 911, Serena continued to watch the boat. Jason hadn't come back out with any more cages. That might mean that he was finished. If that was the case, he might be leaving soon.

She hoped that Cassidy could get here in time.

But if she didn't? What were they going to do? Serena had to think of some way to stop this guy.

"She's on her way," Webster said. "She said she'll be here in ten minutes and don't make any moves."

"But he's about to leave," Serena said.

Webster pushed his glasses up as he stared at the boat at the end of the dock. A little bit of that Superman vibe returned to him. "You're right. That is what it looks like."

"I have an idea," Serena said, explaining it to him. "It's the only thing I can think of."

"Let's give it a try."

They rushed back to the ice cream truck and climbed inside. A moment later, Serena took off down the lane, her music blaring. As she arrived at the house, she pressed on her brakes, put the truck into Park, and stepped out.

She waved her hand. "Isn't it a lovely day here on Lantern Beach? I got a special you're not going to want to miss. One ice cream sandwich for a dollar or five for five dollars."

Webster remained in the truck with Nutty Buddy down on the floor beside him so no one could see him.

Jason narrowed his gaze and stormed over to her. "What are you doing here?"

"I'm selling ice cream. That's what I do."

"But we don't want any. Get out of here."

Serena wasn't done with this yet. "Looks like

you're about to take a trip." She nodded toward the boat.

His gaze darkened. "It's none of your business. Like I said, get out of here."

"You know, I feel bad about what happened yesterday. I'd like to offer you any type of ice cream you want. You just name it."

"I'm lactose intolerant and trying to cut out sugar. Now, scram."

Serena couldn't help but think that this man was talking to her like someone might talk to a stray dog. Her bad feeling about the man continued to grow.

"I'm thinking about getting a boat. Can I take a look at yours?"

Jason stormed closer, his face turning as red as a cherry popsicle. "What part of get out of here don't you understand?"

"Maybe she'll understand this," a new voice said.

Serena slowly turned and saw someone standing by her ice cream truck, gun in hand. She let out a soft gasp.

That was the woman Serena had talked to when she'd been looking for Nutty Buddy's owner that very first day she'd found him—the grandmotherly lady who'd helped with the crab fest and who lived by herself at the end of the lane and who'd called Nutty Buddy a rat.

The problem was she looked anything but sweet right now. Instead, she looked like the matriarch of a crime family.

Webster stepped out of the van with one hand raised and the other clutching Nutty Buddy as Grandma pointed the gun at them.

He mouthed, "I'm sorry."

It was okay. Neither of them had been able to anticipate this. Serena tried to tell him that with her gaze.

"So let's cut to the chase," Webster said. "You guys appear to be running a dog-smuggling ring."

"It's harmless. Nobody gets hurt." Grandma gave them all a cold stare. "Unless they do. You should've stayed out of this."

"Just like Paul Witherspoon did," Serena said.

She glared. "He was different. He was one of us until he suddenly started getting soft. It really was a crying shame."

"He wanted out, so you killed him?" Serena asked. The explanation sounded so heartless.

"It's a long story," Jason said. "We don't have time to talk about it. Now, get the dog. He should go for at least two thousand in the black market."

Serena's eyes went to Nutty Buddy. She couldn't bear the thought of that dog being taken away. She had to do something.

"Paul was the one who called the dogcatcher, wasn't he?" she blurted.

Jason and Grandma looked at her.

"How do you know about that?" Grandma asked, her eyes narrowed.

"I'm just putting the pieces together now, but it makes sense. He needed a way to get out of this without you guys realizing that he was the one who pulled the plug on the operation. That's why he called the dogcatcher."

"That's right," Grandma said, her gun still pointed at Webster. "But when the dogcatcher came, he had nothing to hold us on. As far as he could tell, we weren't doing anything illegal."

"But if that's your dog," Serena pointed to Nutty Buddy. "Why didn't you claim him when I walked up to your house?"

"I couldn't let anybody have any indication I was behind this. I want my hands to be clean."

"So you let your grandson take the fall for you?" Serena nodded to Jason. Now that she thought about it, the two showed some resemblance.

"He's not my grandson. He's my nephew. And Paul Witherspoon was nothing but a namby-pamby whimpering girly-girl of a man. As soon as he saw that one girl on the news crying over her stolen dog, he went all soft on us. He wanted to stop all of this.

But we couldn't let him do that. So Jason did the only thing we could do."

"So he stabbed him?" Serena asked.

"We had no other choice. If that dog hadn't gotten away when it did, the police may have never found Paul in time. We would've had a chance to clean things up," Grandma said. "Now, enough talking. We need to take care of business. All of you, in the boat."

Serena exchanged a glance with Webster. She knew if they got in that boat, they'd never be seen around here again.

She looked back at Grandma. Grandma had a gun. There was very little they could do when that was pointed at them.

Think, Serena. Think.

But she came up with nothing.

Cassidy should be here any minute. That was her only chance.

But did Cassidy even know that this house was back here?

They started walking toward the dock, Serena feeling like they had no choice. Her heart pounded in her chest. She only hoped that Nutty Buddy would be okay. And Webster. Especially since she had gotten him into this.

Right before they stepped on the dock, when

Serena felt like all hope was lost, a new sound cut through the air.

It wasn't a police siren either.

It was Elsa. Playing "The More We Get Together."

The sound threw them off just enough that Webster was able to kick the gun from Grandma's hand. It fired as it flew through the air.

"Run!" Webster shouted.

Serena didn't have to be told twice. She started toward the ice cream truck, knowing she could use it to take cover, if nothing else.

Just as they arrived there, Cassidy pulled up with another police car.

"Freeze!" she shouted. "Put your hands in the air!"

Serena and Webster glanced at each other. Maybe this was really over.

But Serena felt her legs going weak, like ice cream melting on a hot day.

That evening, Serena and Webster sat on the deck outside her camper as the stars began to twinkle overhead. She was waiting for Cassidy to arrive. But her heart felt heavy. She knew that when Cassidy came, she was going to need to turn Nutty Buddy over to her.

She didn't want to let the dog go.

Though Serena knew she'd bonded with the canine, she hadn't realized how deeply that bond already went.

"You did a good job here tonight," Webster said. "All those dogs will go back to their owners. That's something you can be proud of."

"I wish I felt excited." She ran her hand over Nutty Buddy's back. "But all I can think about is sending this boy away."

"Instead of thinking about your loss, think about how happy his owner will be. He's a great dog. I'm sure somebody has really missed him."

"I'm sure you're right." That should make her feel better, but it didn't. Not really.

The rest of the scene at the house at the end of the lane had been crazy. Jason and Grandma had been arrested. Carl from animal control had come to take charge of the dogs. From what Serena was able to overhear, Jason and Grandma had been doing this for a few years now. Serena could only imagine how many dogs had passed between their hands during that time.

Everything seemed surreal.

Just then, Cassidy pulled up and parked her SUV

in front of Serena's lot. There was a grim look on her face as she walked up to the deck. She sat on the edge and looked up at Serena for a moment before saying anything.

"I'm glad you called me tonight," she started. "It could've been an ugly situation."

"I'm glad you showed up when you did."

"It's important that you let me do the policework," Cassidy continued. "I don't want to see you get hurt."

"I just wanted to stop Jason before he left with those dogs."

"I understand," Cassidy said, no judgment in her voice. It was mostly just worry.

"Did all the dogs get returned to their owners?" Webster asked.

"All the owners are on their way to get their dogs," Cassidy said. "They're going to come here to Lantern Beach. It was the easiest way to coordinate things."

Serena rubbed the pup's head again, feeling the burn in her throat as she tried to fight back tears. "And when is Nutty Buddy's owner coming?"

"That's what I wanted to talk to you about."

Serena held her breath, unsure what Cassidy was about to say.

"It turns out that Nutty Buddy's owner was an

elderly woman. She passed away after living a long, full life. This woman's daughter was supposed to come and pick up the dog. But, when she arrived, the dog was no longer there. I'm not sure how Jason heard about everything, but he somehow managed to grab Nutty Buddy before the authorities arrived."

"Do you think he killed the woman?"

"No, I think he just happened to be in the right place at the right time. These guys were opportunists. They heard about dogs they wanted, and then waited for opportunities to grab them."

"So, the woman's daughter is going to come get him?" Serena clarified.

"I actually talked to her myself, and she was going to look for a new home for the dog. I told her that we might have one here in Lantern Beach."

Serena could hardly breathe as she tried to process what Cassidy had just said. "You mean . . ."

Cassidy smiled. "That you can keep the dog if you want."

She let out a little squeal and hugged Nutty Buddy closer. "I would love to have this dog. He feels like my long-lost best friend."

Cassidy's smile grew wider. "I thought you might feel that way."

"But I'm going to have to rename him."

Cassidy and Webster both groaned.

"No, for real this time," Serena said. "This is going to be the last time I do this."

"And what are you going to name him now?" Webster asked.

She looked at the dog and rubbed his ears. "Scoops."

"Scoops?" Cassidy asked.

Serena shrugged. "I thought it was fitting. I mean, I am the ice cream lady, but I am also a reporter who is out getting the scoop. Get it?"

Cassidy and Webster groaned again. But then they chuckled.

"I like it," Webster said.

"Do you know what? I like it too," Cassidy said before standing. "I'm going to get going now. But if you need anything, let me know."

Serena nodded and waved goodbye.

Then it was just her, Webster, and Scoops.

"So, I know things kind of started off rocky between us," Webster said.

"You noticed?" She'd thought he was clueless.

"I just pretended like I didn't for the sake of peace. I know it's weird when somebody new steps into a leadership position. But I'm hoping that you and I will work together. So far, I feel like we're a good team."

Serena wanted to make a smart comeback. But

she wouldn't be true to herself if she did. "You know what? I think we might make a good team too. As long as Scoops is here to help us out."

Webster rubbed the dog's head. "I couldn't agree more."

COMING NEXT: MILKSHAKE UP

ALSO BY CHRISTY BARRITT:

YOU MIGHT ALSO ENJOY ...

THE SQUEAKY CLEAN MYSTERY SERIES

On her way to completing a degree in forensic science, Gabby St. Claire drops out of school and starts her own crime-scene cleaning business. When a routine cleaning job uncovers a murder weapon the police overlooked, she realizes that the wrong person is in jail. She also realizes that crime scene cleaning might be the perfect career for utilizing her investigative skills.

#7 Mucky Streak

#8 Foul Play

#9 Broom & Gloom

#10 Dust and Obey

#11 Thrill Squeaker

#11.5 Swept Away (novella)

#12 Cunning Attractions

#13 Cold Case: Clean Getaway

#14 Cold Case: Clean Sweep

#15 Cold Case: Clean Break

While You Were Sweeping, A Riley Thomas Spinoff

THE LANTERN BEACH SERIES:

LANTERN BEACH MYSTERIES

A notorious gang puts a bounty on Detective Cady Matthews's head after she takes down their leader, leaving her no choice but to hide until she can testify at trial. But her temporary home across the country on a remote North Carolina island isn't as peaceful as she initially thinks. Living under the new identity of Cassidy Livingston, she struggles to keep her investigative skills tucked away. But Cassidy is supposed to be keeping a low profile. One wrong move could lead to both her discovery and her demise. Can she bring justice to the island . . . or will the hidden currents surrounding her pull her under for good?

Hidden Currents

Flood Watch

Storm Surge

Dangerous Waters

Perilous Riptide

Deadly Undertow

LANTERN BEACH ROMANTIC SUSPENSE

Tides of Deception

Shadow of Intrigue

Storm of Doubt

Winds of Danger

Rains of Remorse

LANTERN BEACH PD

On the Lookout

Attempt to Locate

First Degree Murder

Dead on Arrival

Plan of Action

THE WORST DETECTIVE EVER:

I'm not really a private detective. I just play one on TV.

Joey Darling, better known to the world as Raven Remington, detective extraordinaire, is trying to separate herself from her invincible alter ego. She played the spunky character for five years on the hit TV show *Relentless*, which catapulted her to fame and into the role of Hollywood's sweetheart. When her marriage falls apart, her finances dwindle to nothing, and her father disappears, Joey finds herself on the Outer Banks of North Carolina, trying to piece together her life away from the limelight. But as people continually mistake her for the character she played on TV, she's tasked with solving real life crimes . . . even though she's terrible at it.

#1 Ready to Fumble

#2 Reign of Error

#3 Safety in Blunders

#4 Join the Flub

#5 Blooper Freak

#6 Flaw Abiding Citizen

#7 Gaffe Out Loud

#8 Joke and Dagger

#9 Wreck the Halls

#10 Glitch and Famous (coming soon)

ABOUT THE AUTHOR

USA Today has called Christy Barritt's books "scary, funny, passionate, and quirky."

Christy writes both mystery and romantic suspense novels that are clean with underlying messages of faith. Her books have won the Daphne du Maurier Award for Excellence in Suspense and Mystery, have been twice nominated for the Romantic Times Reviewers' Choice Award, and have finaled for both a Carol Award and Foreword Magazine's Book of the Year.

She is married to her Prince Charming, a man who thinks she's hilarious—but only when she's not trying to be. Christy is a self-proclaimed klutz, an avid music lover who's known for spontaneously bursting into song, and a road trip aficionado.

When she's not working or spending time with her family, she enjoys singing, playing the guitar, and exploring small, unsuspecting towns where people have no idea how accident-prone she is.

Find Christy online at:

www.christybarritt.com
www.facebook.com/christybarritt
www.twitter.com/cbarritt

Sign up for Christy's newsletter to get information on all of her latest releases here: **www.christybarritt.com/newsletter-sign-up/**

If you enjoyed this book, please consider leaving a review.